From out of the blue she kissed him

Her lips touched  sh of air, so soft the ible for him to pull aw and his breath caugh

He hadn't expected this, hadn't been prepared for it. He'd dreamed of it, though, of kissing her and holding her and learning her by heart. His dreams hadn't done this justice.

That thought took root inside his skull, unfurling until it broke through the clouds in his mind.

He'd dreamed of this.

The realization had him stiffening and dragging his mouth from hers. Feeling guilty.

Desire and honor warred within him. He wanted to kiss her again, to breathe her in, to draw her up and lay her down.

"April."

"I know. I shouldn't have done that."

He shouldn't have done that. He'd told himself just this afternoon he wouldn't. He'd promised. And not just himself.

Dear Reader,

When I begin a book, somehow I already know the first words of my story. Although it's completely unexplainable, it feels like a gentle current from an invisible source, and it's one of the things I love most about writing. I also love the music that plays through my mind throughout a story's telling. In *A Man of His Word*, the song I kept humming was "Life Is a Highway." I'm pretty sure it's the favorite song of Cole Cavanaugh, the man of his word in *A Man of His Word*.

See what I mean? Completely unexplainable.

As I was writing the first words in the first story I set in Orchard Hill, Michigan, I had no idea there would be others. I simply felt the current and started down that highway. I'm so pleased you opened *A Man of His Word*, dear reader, and are about to share a little part of this hilly and winding highway with me.

In everything you do, safe travels.

Until next time and always,

Sandra Steffen

A Man of His Word

—

Sandra Steffen

⟨H⟩ **HARLEQUIN**® SPECIAL EDITION

Recycling programs
for this product may
not exist in your area.

ISBN-13: 978-1-335-57417-6

A Man of His Word

Copyright © 2019 by Sandra E. Steffen

Printed in U.S.A.

Sandra Steffen is an award-winning, bestselling author of more than thirty-seven novels. Honored to have won a RITA® Award, a National Readers' Choice Award and a Wish Award, her most cherished regards come from readers around the world. She married her high school sweetheart and raised four sons while simultaneously pursuing her dream of publication. She loves to laugh, read, take long walks and have long talks with friends, and write, write, write.

Books by Sandra Steffen

Harlequin Special Edition

Round-the-Clock Brides

A Bride Until Midnight
A Bride Before Dawn
A Bride by Summer
A Man of His Word

The Wedding Gift

In loving memory of my sister, Deanna.
I miss you every day, Dee,
and I hope your paths are lined with daisies
that are as beautiful as you are.

For Kinsley, my eighth wonder,
and for the first seven, Anora, Leah,
Landen, Anna, Erin, Dalton and Brynn—
God's blessings, each and every one of you.

Chapter One

Go see her.

In the beginning, the thought had been little more than a whisper on Cole Cavanaugh's pillow, but lately it had grown more insistent. Like a mosquito, it was a nuisance when it was buzzing in his ear, disconcerting when it wasn't.

Go see her.

He'd grown accustomed to the notion. And adept at pushing it back. For eight months, he'd been pushing it back. And still the idea persisted.

Go see her. Go see her. Go see her.

It had thundered in the night, but instead of rain, morning had dawned to a ceiling of fog that hung above the Genesee River, stretching out over the gradual rises along its banks. Standing in the thick of it, it was easy for Cole to imagine that the hazy white dome encompassed all of upstate New York, stretching throughout all of New England, even inching to the Great Lakes and into Michigan.

Where she lived.

Here on the hillside just outside Rochester, the fog shrouded the peaks of the rafters of the mansion Cole and his business partner, Grant Maloney, were constructing on this expansive piece of riverfront property. Former roommates, they'd come a long way from the decks, garages, family room additions and bungalows they'd built fresh out of college twelve years ago. This beauty would be a notch in their tool belts for sure.

Cole and Grant stood together this morning, watching as their clients, a wealthy middle-aged couple with a mile-long list of must-haves and a grown daughter, meandered away from them to their Tesla SUV, deep in excited conversation about their future home. Cole had already given his skilled carpenters the signal to get back to work. Power saws screeched and nail guns fired. Around back a skid steer rumbled as it lifted another pallet of stone from the bed of a lowboy trailer.

Go see her. Go see her.

When he'd first had the thought, he'd been in the recovery room in the VA hospital, delirious from pain medication. *Go see her.* He hadn't, of course. It would be months before he walked again. Besides, it was too soon. Jay had been gone only six months then. Surely April was still reeling. God knew Cole was.

That hadn't kept him from thinking about what he would say. If he ever did say anything. *Go see her.*

Through the months of grueling physical therapy that had followed, the thought came unbidden, again and again. He'd been pushed and bullied by the meanest therapist that ever lived, but no one pushed him harder than he pushed himself. Adeline, his therapist, cried the first time Cole made it to the top of the stairs on his own. That landing represented the fruit of his labor, his determination and hard work.

Go see her. Go see her. Go see her.

For the first time, he'd considered it. But the timing still wasn't right. Nothing felt quite right since Jay had died on the battlefield. So instead of going to see Jay's widow, Cole finished rehab, then returned to Rochester where he delved back into the booming business he and Grant had started.

Go see her go see her go see her go see her go see—

"See her?" The deep timbre of Grant Maloney's voice cut into Cole's reverie. With sound carrying uncommonly far in this fog, Grant kept his voice intentionally low. "She looks just as good coming as she does going."

Cole glanced askance at his friend, who was watching the leggy beauty climb into her father's Tesla right now. "I know. She just spoke to me."

"My point, pal. You saw her, but you didn't *see* her. If you had, you would have written your cell number on the back of that business card she just asked you for. By the end of the day she would be calling you, probably to invite you over for a drink, among other things."

Cole shook his head lightly. "Not even you would mix this kind of business with that kind of pleasure."

Grant smiled, for his blue eyes, ripped body and outgoing personality left him with no shortage of women asking for his phone number. "True," he said. "But I would have thought about it, fantasized about it long and hard first."

Cole's fantasies ran in another direction. *Go see her. Go see her. GO SEE HER.*

They each took a call, Cole from their electrician and Grant from their office manager. They both had building projects to quote and papers littering their desks and emails to answer and schedules to adjust and solutions to find. In other words, they had work to do. With that in mind, they started toward Cole's company truck.

On the way, Cole said, "There's something I need to talk to you about."

Grant eyed his friend. "You look serious. Dead serious. I hope that means what I think it means. If you're finally going to see her, it's about damn time is all I can say."

A month ago Cole had made the mistake of telling Grant about Jay, and about the dream Cole had had of April when he'd been wounded the second time. "That's the price I pay for telling you anything. But yes. I am. I'm going to see her."

"When do you leave?" Grant matched his stride to the friend he admired more than he said aloud.

Cole appreciated that. Admiration made him uneasy. "As soon as I tie up loose ends here."

"Tomorrow then," Grant said, opening the passenger door.

"You're impossible," Cole declared.

Grant chuckled. "I couldn't have landed this deal without you."

Cole drove slowly through the fog, and Grant's tone grew more serious. "We're well into construction now. I'll take it from here for as long as I need to, like I did when you were overseas. Keep your phone and your laptop close. I'm glad you're going, Cole. It might just be the only way you're going to find peace. Maybe it'll bring her a little peace, too."

In his mind, Cole pictured long curling hair, full lips and golden brown eyes. He hadn't actually met April Avery, but he felt as if he had, for he swore he remembered her face, her eyes especially, and the glimmer in them that was hope. That glimmer of hope had reached thousands of miles to the other side of the world eight months ago when he'd been on the precipice of death.

What would he say to her? What did a man say to the widow of his battlefield brother?

Would making this trip bring either of them peace? The notion lodged in Cole's mind, in his throat, in the middle of his chest. He drove with the windows down. And took what felt like the first deep breath he'd drawn in a very long time.

Cole stopped at the curb at 404 Baldwin Street in Orchard Hill, Michigan, then sat for interminable seconds, his foot on the brake and his mouth suddenly bone-dry.

He knew he could do an about-face and follow the route he'd taken back to Rochester, or he could fire up his GPS, or open the road map lying on the seat next to him or just wing it and head someplace else. Anyplace else. But he also knew, even as thoughts of retreat formed, that he wasn't going anywhere.

He didn't know how long he would be here, but it was possible his stay would be extended. It hadn't taken him long to tie up those loose ends back in New York. The moment he had, he'd stuffed some clothes into two duffel bags, tossed everything next to his tools in the back of his truck, put his laptop on the seat next to him and drove to Michigan.

The flowers growing in wild disarray beside the sidewalk seemed as familiar to him as the orchards he'd passed north of town and the old stone church just inside the city limit sign. Everything looked exactly as Jay had described. He half expected Jay to meet him halfway down the driveway. But Jay couldn't, of course, and the knowledge cut like a knife.

Getting out at the curb, Cole made sure both feet were firmly underneath him before he took his first step, something he did almost without conscious thought now. His legs carried him unfalteringly up the sidewalk only to stop for no good reason, his feet planting themselves on the concrete in front of the stoop.

He knew what bravery was, how it felt and what it meant. And yet he stood in the dappled shade of an enormous maple tree, his insides quaking. Releasing a deep breath, he went over potential scenarios again.

As he felt in his back pocket for the sheet of paper he'd brought with him, his ears picked up sounds of children's giggles and a gentle, melodious voice coming from inside the house. The next thing he knew, he was at the door. If not for the twinge in his left thigh, he might have believed he'd willed himself up onto the stoop where a sturdy screen door was all that separated him from the family inside.

His rap on the door silenced the giggles and started a stampede of small feet. Closer now, that melodious voice firmly called, "Girls, wait for me."

An instant later April Avery was looking at him through the screen, a little girl on either side of her. Her light brown hair was long and curly, her nose pert, her eyes—he stopped there, halted by the expression in their depths.

"It's you," she said, her voice quavering.

So she recognized him, too.

The warm August breeze rustled the leaves overhead. Someone on the block was mowing a lawn. A car drove by, voices called, a dog barked. To everyone else in the neighborhood, this was probably an ordinary summer day.

"I should have called, ma'am," he said, feeling more like a soldier again than a civilian, his back ramrod straight, shoulders squared, gaze direct. "But I thought… That is…" He swallowed and mentally gave himself a swift kick. "I'm Cole Cavanaugh," he said, because whether she recognized him or not, and vice versa, this was the first time they'd actually met. "Hello, April. Or would you prefer I call you Mrs. Avery?"

"Gosh, no. April's fine."

"You know him, Mama?" one of the twins asked. Cole realized it was Violet. Jay had told all the guys in their unit about his little girls, and told countless stories. This one was definitely Violet.

Since April seemed to be having trouble speaking, too, Cole glanced down at the little girl who'd asked the question. Violet Avery's curly brown hair was held away from her cherubic face with a plastic tiara, her eyes golden brown, like her mother's. The child was staring at him now.

Before the silence became any more uncomfortable, he told her, "I'm a friend of your dad's."

He tried swallowing. Failing that, he managed to take a deep breath, for more than a year had passed and he still found himself speaking of Jay in the present tense.

"Our daddy's dead," the other little girl said in a voice softer than her sister's. Despite the pink feather boa she wore, Gracie Avery looked so much like her father Cole couldn't take his eyes off her.

"He's in heaven, with the angels," she added reverently, her face heart-shaped, her hair blond and her gray eyes serious.

"Yes, I know."

"You believe in heaven?" Violet cut in. "'Cuz Maddie next door is seven and says there's no such thing."

Almost five now, both girls waited with rapt attention for Cole's reply. Hoping his smile appeared more natural than it felt, he nodded at them before once again training his gaze on their mother. At almost thirty, she was a stunner wrapped in a wholesome girl-next-door persona. It was those eyes, that smile, that trim, curvy body.

"I do," he said. "Believe, I mean, in heaven. I've seen a lot of, er, things—" He'd almost told a four-year-old he'd seen hell up close. "There must be a heaven, I mean. I think there is."

He clamped his mouth shut. For goodness' sake, he co-owned a successful business, had a Purple Heart, an invitation to ride in more parades than he could shake a stick at and an inbox full of propositions from women he hadn't even met. Since when did he have trouble conversing in complete sentences?

"He's a friend of Daddy's," Violet said loudly. "Let 'im in, Mama."

"Yes, Mama, you should let him in."

Violet's bossiness and Grace's practically were both wasted. April Avery was already opening the door.

April happened to breathe in as Cole Cavanaugh walked through the door she held. His scent wasn't pronounced, carrying only a faint trace of spruce and peppermint. Jay had smelled like spring, like brisk breezes and sprouts of green grass peeking through the last patch of snow. Which had nothing to do with anything. She needed to gather her wits, stop sniffing strangers and say something intelligent.

Nothing came to mind.

She continued to stare up at her visitor, trying to wrap her mind around a simple, stark fact: the tall rugged man now standing in her living room had been on the battlefield with her husband the day he died. Calling upon her good manners, she drew the twins closer and said, "These are my daughters, Gracie and Violet. Girls, this is Mr. Cavanaugh."

"Cole," he said abruptly. And then, as if he hadn't intended to be so forceful, his eyes went from April's to each of the girls'. "Not even my father answered to Mr. Cavanaugh. If it's all right with the three of you, I prefer to be called Cole."

She noticed he didn't smile.

Bits and pieces of descriptions Jay had mentioned in his video calls, emails and letters filtered across April's mind. One night early into his tour of duty he'd told her not to worry too much because there was a guy in his unit named Cole Cavanaugh who had his back.

"C.C. has listening down to an art form," Jay had said, his handsome face slightly blurry on the computer screen. "Picture Clint Eastwood's piercing stare in those old *Dirty Harry* movies my dad loves to this day. When he wants to, C.C. can duplicate the raspy voice. But he's a dreamer at heart. At first he took a lot of ribbing from the guys in our unit over it, but the second time a dream he had helped us avoid a deadly ambush, the ribbing turned into some serious respect."

A dreamer herself, April had been intrigued. She'd slept better that night knowing that Cole Cavanaugh was with her husband on the other side of the world.

"Cole, and not C.C.?" she asked the former soldier standing before her today.

The shrug of his broad shoulders was surprisingly sheepish for someone made of sharp angles, corded muscles and a gaze that missed nothing. "Jay is the only person who ever got away with calling me C.C."

With a small smile, she said, "You may call him Cole if you'd like, girls."

Violet clapped her hands as she turned to her sister. "Think we should, Gracie?"

Slightly taller than her twin, Grace remained quiet for so long April wasn't sure she was going to grant Cole's wish. Finally the imp nodded and it was settled.

Violet shook her head dramatically. "It took you long enough." With that, the two began asking Cole Cavanaugh questions about what was better, princesses or fairies, purple or pink, butterflies or fireflies, and so on.

These two, April thought on an indulgent smile. She never knew what one or the other was going to say. Cole was doing his best to answer the deluge of questions diplomatically. It gave April an opportunity to study him.

His hair was as dark as fresh-ground coffee. Given the chance to grow a little longer, it would probably be wavy. His eyes were a medium brown, the bones in his face sharply sculpted, forehead, brows, jaw and chin. Judging by the slight hollowness in his cheeks and the loose fit of his clothes, he'd dropped some weight recently. It made her wonder how long he'd been out of the army, for he'd gone back into battle after—

Everything inside April went utterly still, as if moving so much as a fraction of an inch might cleave the fragile scab on the wound she'd sustained from losing Jay. Cole Cavanaugh had fought beside Jay, had lived beside him, had nearly died beside him. He'd saved Jay's life time and again.

Except that day, fourteen months ago, when Jay saved his.

Gracie and Violet had been just over three and a half then—too young to understand what was happening. And yet they'd sensed that something tragic had occurred. Climbing onto the sofa, they'd sat pressed tight together, wide-eyed and silent as the house began to fill with people.

April couldn't allow her mind to travel to that bleak day, couldn't relive the waiting and praying, the cloying dread; she couldn't let her memory dwell upon the blur of minutes, hours and days that had followed the incomprehensible words that had changed her world forever.

She closed her eyes. When she opened them, she was in the present once again on this Tuesday afternoon in early August. She heard Gracie ask Cole if he would like to watch her new princess movie with her. At the same time Violet invited him to a tea party instead.

Poor Cole looked to April for help.

"Girls," she said. "Mr. Cavan—Cole isn't here to watch a movie or have a tea party today."

His warrior's face showed his relief. She offered him a smile, for her daughters could be overwhelming. She seemed to remember Jay mentioning that Cole didn't have any family to speak of. He probably wasn't accustomed to the antics of young children.

"Why is he here, then?" Gracie asked in her straightforward way.

April glanced at Cole, thinking, *Out of the mouths of babes*. Why *was* he here?

His apparent loss for words brought a wave of apprehension to the pit of her stomach. She'd heard from two of the other guys in Jay's old unit, and had learned that Cole Cavanaugh had been injured in the same battle that claimed Jay's life. She suspected that had something to do with the reason Cole was here.

"Gracie, let's put in your new princess movie, and Violet, get your teacups and saucers. You may watch your movie while you both enjoy a spot of pretend magical tea."

The two turned to one another, their eyes meeting in silent twin-speak. "We don't wanna," they said in unison.

Oh, dear. Enticing them to give the adults a little privacy would require some serious finesse. In the end, they couldn't resist the alternative April offered them: an ice cream treat while they painted a picture for Cole so he would remember them when he left.

And so, with her children busily painting with watercolors in the shade on the patio, April led Cole back inside. Once her eyes had readjusted to the dim light in her kitchen, she found herself staring up at him. He was taller than Jay, and she was certain she'd never seen anyone who could hold so still.

All of a sudden, he shifted his weight from one hip to the other, as if to relieve pain. It reminded her that Jay wasn't the only one injured by this horrible war. Not that she ever truly forgot. "You were there with him, at the end?" she whispered.

His throat convulsed, but he nodded.

Gathering her wits about her, she said, "Would you like something to drink? Water? Iced tea? A pop?"

"Do you happen to have ginger ale?"

That had been Jay's favorite soft drink, too, one of many preferences the two men had shared. She shook her head.

"Water's good."

She took two bottles from the refrigerator and handed him one of them. Cole opened the cap and took a drink.

Noticing him shifting his weight from one hip to the other again, she said, "Would you like to sit down?"

He glanced around the kitchen, through the screen door into the backyard, then back at April. "I've been driving for hours. It feels good to move around. Your house is exactly the way Jay described it," he said, his brown eyes softening as he looked into hers. "Would you mind showing me the rest?"

It was an odd request, but what about learning to live without Jay these past fourteen months had been normal? "Jay talked about our house?" she asked.

"When he got especially homesick he used to talk about his life here," Cole said. "He told me about this kitchen and how he put that nick in the floor, and the bathroom with its 1950s pink tile, and he said Gracie and Violet communicated without saying a word. If I hadn't just witnessed it with my own two eyes, I wouldn't have believed it."

"They know him from his pictures and the stories they hear," April said quietly. "But they barely remember him anymore." She hadn't meant to say that, and imagined Cole could tell that from her wide-eyed expression. Perhaps because he didn't spout any of the trite platitudes people often felt they needed to say at times like this, April heard herself ask, "Did he suffer?"

Something flickered through his eyes, but his gaze didn't falter, and neither did his voice as he said, "The bullet severed a main artery. If he was in pain, he didn't show it."

Cole didn't have to close his eyes to see the blood, his and Jay's, seeping into the dirt underneath them. A bullet had pierced Cole's right side. The pain had been searing, but it was a scratch compared to Jay's injury. He'd tried desperately to quell the flow of Jay's blood. Told him to stay with him, that help was on the way. But Cole had known it was no use. Jay had known it, too. His voice fading to a rasp, Jay had whispered, "Tell April I—"

Fourteen months later, Cole said, "He was indescribably calm. You were his final thought."

Blinking back tears, she whispered, "The jerk."

Cole did a double take, for that was the last thing he'd expected.

"He said he'd come back," she said, going to the door and peering out. "He promised."

He could see Gracie and Violet through the screen. They talked nonstop at a round glass-topped table, and although he couldn't quite make out their words, he could see they were busily painting a picture for him. Gracie was dipping her brush into pastels while Violet painted her sky a bright vivid blue.

"You'd like to see the rest of the house, you said?"

April asked after she'd taken a moment to regain her composure.

He nodded. And if she'd thought it was an odd request, which it probably was, she didn't say it out loud.

"As you can see, this is the kitchen," she said, gesturing with one hand.

She moved on briskly. Perhaps she preferred to keep moving, too.

"You saw the living room and foyer when you arrived, but here it is again. The fireplace is a godsend in the winter. And here's the hall." She pointed at an open door directly ahead of them. "The only bathroom."

She turned to the right, and Cole followed her into a small pink bedroom containing two beds with matching comforters, the floor strewn with dolls and books and magic wands and costumes with frothy skirts.

"Jay built these beds with his own two hands," she said. "He sanded the wood until it was so smooth there wasn't a single sliver that could pierce the girls' tender skin. We painted them together a few weeks before he was scheduled to leave. Gosh, we couldn't wait to show the twins their new bunk beds. After a week of their arguing and fighting over who got to sleep on the top bunk, Jay took the beds apart and arranged them side by side. A wise man."

Perhaps the most beautiful smile Cole had ever witnessed softened April's pink lips. She bustled past him, but stopped short of the doorway of the last room on this floor. From behind her Cole could see two dressers, a bedside table and a large bed with pillows on only one side.

"This was our room," she said. She took a few steps away then glanced back at him. "One month to the day after he died, I dragged our mattress outside and put a match to it along with the *Seven Steps of Grief* pamphlet some kind soul with the best of intentions gave me."

"You burned your bed?" Cole asked.

She shrugged. "Jay promised he'd come back. Promised. The flames were high and I'd never seen so much black smoke. I cried so hard I thought I was going to have a stroke. My sister says I was lucky the neighbors didn't call the fire department. She thinks I've gotten stuck in the anger stage of grief."

What was he supposed to say to that? Cole wondered. Her gaze locked with his, and she clamped her hand over her mouth. Lowering it, she said, "You must think I'm certifiable. I'm not. I loved Jay with my whole heart. I still do."

He believed her. "He felt the same way about you. And the twins. A change came over him when he talked about the three of you. I could see it, hear it. We all could."

"He talked about us? What did he tell you?" she asked, intrigued.

"Oh. Everyday things. He wasn't like some of the guys. Jay wouldn't give any intimate details, no matter how much the guys badgered him. He told us about the day he met you, how he proposed, how you both danced in the rain on your wedding day. He recalled the first time he held the girls, how you both knew this was the house you wanted to live in forever."

There was such wistfulness in her smile. And Cole wondered if it would be too forward to ask her to show him the upstairs. Because Jay had told him about the space, and how it was unfinished, and how he'd planned to turn it into a master sanctuary as soon as he came home.

Cole could picture the before and after Jay had described. For months now he'd had an idea in the back of his mind. He'd never planned to act on it, but now that he was here, he wondered what she would say if he brought it up. First he had to take a look at it.

"What about the upstairs?" he asked. "Jay talked about it a lot, about the plans the two of you had for it. I'm a builder, and I'd sure like to see it."

Surprise widened her golden brown eyes. She stuck her hands on her hips, the action drawing his gaze to her narrow waist covered by the thin fabric of her summer dress. Not quite five-five in her flat sandals, she was pretty but she was no weakling.

She peeked at the girls again then led the way back to the living room and up the open staircase on the far wall. They went through a door at the top and emerged into an empty, stiflingly hot, wide-open space.

Typical of Cape Cod-style houses, the roof sloped to shoulder-high walls on two sides. The overhead rafters were exposed, the floor covered in dusty rough-sawn oak. Light spilled through windows on either end, as well as through two larger windows in the dormers on the front of the house. Stained batted insulation was falling down in places.

A blank canvas, Jay had called it. Cole didn't have to close his eyes to envision his best friend's plans for this space.

"Jay wasn't exaggerating," he said. "It has a great deal of potential."

"You've seen enough?" she asked.

He nodded, and she preceded him through the door, the hem of her dress brushing his jeans-clad knee as she passed. Steeling himself against her feminine softness, he leaned heavily on the railing as he descended the stairs, reaching the bottom just as April disappeared into the kitchen to check on Violet and Gracie again.

"Time can drag when you're holed up in a bunker in the middle of the desert," he said, following. "The boredom is almost unbearable. Jay passed a lot of that time talking about room sizes, custom closets and a luxurious bathroom with a walk-in shower for two. Just about every guy in our unit weighed in on claw-foot bathtubs versus the jetted kind."

He took the CAD drawing from his back pocket, unfolded it and handed it to April. "Is this the way you remember your plans? Yours and Jay's?"

The drawing shook slightly in her hands, but she kept her eyes cast downward.

"Tell me if I got any of the details wrong," Cole said, although he was pretty sure he hadn't missed anything.

Assuming the slight shake of her head meant the computer drawing he'd designed based on Jay's descriptions was accurate, Cole said, "If you'll let me, I'd like to do it."

"Do what?" she asked.

He hadn't intended to be standing so close when he had this conversation, but he found he couldn't bring himself to move away. From here he could smell the papaya scent of her shampoo, could see the faint dusting of freckles on the tops of her shoulders bared by her sleeveless dress. Her collarbones were narrow, her chin delicate, her mouth pretty, but it was the golden flecks in her light brown eyes he studied the longest.

It occurred to him that he was staring, and he realized she'd asked him a question. In answer, he finally said, "I'd like to finish the upstairs for Jay, and for you and the girls. Time and materials will be part of my gift."

"No."

She surprised him with her vehemence. He waited for her to say more, but that was it. No explanation. Just "no." Coupled with the lift of her chin and the giant step she took away from him, it spoke volumes.

"No?" The breeze carried Grace and Violet's voices into the room from outdoors. April looked at him the way he imagined she looked at her children when they asked a stupid question. He hadn't been expecting an out-and-out refusal.

"Jay couldn't make this a reality. He wanted to more than anything, but he couldn't. I can, April. I'm a licensed contractor and am part owner of a construction company in Rochester, New York. Jay planned to do this for you. His descriptions got us through endless nights of explosions. He dreamed of coming home, of turning his dream for the second story into a reality, and sometimes I dreamed right along with him, back when I used to dream, that is."

He clamped his mouth shut. Damn, he hadn't meant to divulge that little jewel.

"You stopped dreaming?" she asked before she could stop herself.

He expelled a long breath of air. "It's not a big deal."

"When did you stop?" she asked.

He closed his eyes for a moment. "It doesn't matter," he said. "It's nothing."

"Jay called you a dreamer. But that was—" she paused "—before?"

He looked at her. Finally nodded. When she handed the print back to him, he put it on the counter next to his water and said, "I don't have PTSD like a lot of former soldiers. What they go through is hell. I don't dream anymore." He didn't know how they'd gotten on this subject, but he was positive he didn't want to talk about this. "I'd really like you to think about the upstairs. You wouldn't have to worry about a thing. Like I said, it won't cost you anything. You wouldn't even know I'm here except for the hammering and the screeching saws."

She looked at him so long he geared up for her to tell him she had things to do, thanks for dropping by and have a good life. But instead, she said, "I'll need references, and photographs of your work."

He started. Falling back on professionalism, he said, "I can have them for you ASAP."

"Monday is soon enough."

"Why don't we make it Friday, if it's all the same to you." And then, because he was a sucker for punishment, he asked, "What changed your mind?"

"I haven't changed my mind. I never said you couldn't do the job. I haven't said you could, either, but *if* I decide to let you do this, I'll be paying for it."

"April, I know how little a soldier's widow is compensated each month. I can afford this."

"Good for you. But as I said, *if* everything checks out, and if I decide to hire you to finish the upstairs, I'll pay for the renovations. I'll want those references, photos and a detailed quote. I'll get a second bid from an area builder, so don't skimp on your own salary."

A stare down ensued.

She was the one who broke the silence. "*If* I decide to proceed with this, you would be doing it for Jay?"

He nodded, and his throat closed up. In reality, he

would be doing it for Jay, April, Gracie and Violet, too. But it started with Jay.

"I'll think about it," she said. "Meanwhile, I want to see that quote and whatever else you show prospective clients."

He imagined she would run a background check on him—young mothers couldn't be too careful these days. And there was no guarantee she was going to go through with this. But he would work up a quote, present her with sketches, designs, photographs and references. If all went well, she would like it enough to let him begin. And maybe, just maybe, after this project was finished, he would close his eyes at night without seeing death. Perhaps he would stop waking up with a start, when he slept at all. Maybe once he saw Jay's beautiful family settled comfortably into their newly remodeled home, Cole would learn to live with the knowledge that the wrong man had died.

Thirty-three minutes after arriving in Orchard Hill, Cole was back in his black Ford 4x4. The slightly damp paintings from Violet and Gracie were on the bucket seat next to him.

Absently rubbing his sore thigh, Cole remembered when Jay had shown him artwork his daughters had sent him, but he'd failed to mention how stubborn April was. Cole couldn't help wondering what else his best friend had left out.

There was no reason on God's green earth for Cole to feel as if a weight was lifting. It was a little early for that, and yet he was pretty sure a half smile tugged one corner of his mouth up. Toward heaven.

Chapter Two

"Tell me you aren't actually considering hiring him."

April padded quietly through her home, her sister's voice insistent in her ear. Moonlight slanted through the windows on the east side of the house, the late night breeze a caress along the skin on her arms and legs not covered by her short pajamas.

Marilee called from her loft in Denver every Thursday. They'd always been close, but after Jay died these phone calls had come to mean even more to April.

She stopped at the kitchen sink, rinsed out a glass and switched off the overhead light. Like Gracie and Violet, April and her only sister were as different as night and day. In spite of that and the miles that separated them, or perhaps because of those things, they'd always been close.

"I'm serious, April. You don't even know him. I

mean, yes, he bravely served our country and was Jay's best friend, two truly commendable attributes. But hire him out of the blue to finish your upstairs when you had no intention of tackling such a big headache?"

Tonight, April wished she hadn't answered the phone.

"Yes, he's a decorated war hero, Marilee. But in ways I can't explain, he was closer to Jay than his own brothers, and you and I both know how strong his bond was with them."

"I miss him, too," Marilee murmured. "It'll never feel right—his dying, I mean."

Even the house sighed.

April left the kitchen and wandered into the living room, her steps falling lightly on the hardwood floor. "I'm still here," she whispered. "If I don't say anything it's because I'm checking on the girls."

Marilee continued to list all the reasons April should be ultracautious about hiring Cole Cavanaugh to turn her unused upstairs into living space. Only half listening, April entered her daughters' room where moonlight sprinkled like fairy dust onto the floor, its shimmery glow illuminating the two little princesses who were fast asleep.

Gracie lay on her back, the tattered ears of her favorite stuffed rabbit held lovingly in her right hand. On the other bed Violet lay on her side, one little arm dangling over the edge of her mattress. April marveled at their perfection: their hair mussed, their bow lips parted slightly, their unbelievably long eyelashes casting faint shadows on their cheeks.

They'd grown so much this past year. Soon they would be starting school, losing their baby teeth, following their own hearts and finding their own direction. Jay was missing so much. The enormity of it brought a lump to April's throat and an almost unbearable ache to her chest.

She pressed a light kiss to each of the girls' foreheads and breathed them in. As different as they were, they were both summer: raspberries and dandelions, nests made of fluff and warm, soft rain.

With her sister's voice a steady hum in her ear, she gently drew a light throw over each of them. Gracie sighed, and Violet wiggled. By morning her throw would be on the floor.

"Just because he fought next to Jay doesn't mean you should trust him with a nail gun," Marilee insisted.

April didn't bother reminding her only sister that Cole Cavanaugh was a licensed contractor who appeared to be as reputable and honorable as she'd expected any best friend of Jay's to be. "I don't recall asking you if I should trust him," she whispered, pulling the door partway shut behind her.

"I knew it. You trust him. I know you. You take one look at a person and your mind is made up. You're too nice for your own good."

April rolled her eyes as she wandered back out to the living room. She stood at the bottom of the stairs and considered going up, but it was airless and dusty up there and she was barefoot. Besides, she didn't need to see the second floor to know what she was going to do.

"For your information," she told her sister, "I had a background check run on him."

"And?"

She thought about the email she'd received from Sam Lafferty that very afternoon. According to the report from the private investigator Marsh, Reed and Noah Sullivan had hired to find the mother of the baby boy they'd discovered on their doorstep last summer, Cole Cavanaugh grew up in northern Ohio.

"His mother passed away when he was fifteen, and his father died a few years later," April told her sister. "After college he moved to upstate New York where a great uncle of his lived. Other than a couple of speeding tickets in his early twenties, his record is squeaky clean. No wives, past or present, no children, no siblings. He co-owns a successful construction company with a friend from college, has more than one medal of valor and was gravely wounded twice. According to the report, the second time very nearly cost him his left leg and his life. Shall I go on?"

"That's some background check."

April nodded. "Sam Lafferty was very thorough."

"Sam? That's who ran the check? Why didn't you say so? Did he mention me?"

After making sure the front and back doors were locked, April entered her bedroom. "Why would Sam mention you? Don't tell me you slept with him, too."

"Actually, I didn't. I happened to meet Sam at Bell's Tavern, but I was in Orchard Hill because Jay died and I needed to be there with you and the girls and he was about to fly somewhere or other for one of his clients. So no, nothing happened between Sam and me. Pity, that. But we're not talking about me," came Marilee's droll response. "I just don't know about this Cole Cavanaugh. He's carrying a lot of baggage, justifiably so, but I'm afraid for you, April. I worry about you."

April sighed. God save her from all the people who loved her and worried about her.

Her windows were dark behind the slatted blinds, for moonlight hadn't reached this portion of the sky yet. She turned on the lamp on her bedside table and sighed. She didn't need moonlight to bring on her melancholy.

"So," Marilee said, breaking into her reverie. "Are you going to tell me or aren't you?"

"Tell you what?"

"What is Cole Cavanaugh like?"

"I did tell you. I described his hair and eye color, how well he knew Jay."

"But what did he smell like?" Marilee persisted.

Marilee knew her and all her quirks. April knew Marilee just as well, and knew she'd get no peace until she answered her sister's question.

"If you must know, he's winter."

Some people saw eyes first. Some never forgot a face. Others remembered voices. She'd heard of people who recognized others from their walk or the way they laughed. April associated people with certain scents. It wasn't conscious. It just happened. And Cole was winter.

"Remind me, what does winter smell like again?"

April rolled her eyes as if her older sister was sitting on her childhood bed across their room in the house in the Detroit suburbs where they grew up. "You live in Denver and know good and well what winter smells like. But fine, I'll tell you. He's boughs of spruce and a hint of peppermint and snowflakes floating on faint rays of buttery sunlight."

She found herself standing behind her bedroom door where a navy blue robe still hung. Her fingers glided over the lapel, her nose automatically nuzzling the soft fabric. Tears stung her eyes, for Jay's scent was fading. And there wasn't a single thing she could do about it.

"April are you still there?"

Her sister's voice brought April back to their conversation. "I'm here."

"Why do the upstairs now?" Marilee asked. "You haven't been able to bring yourself to change anything, other than your mattress."

"A nice sister wouldn't bring that up."

"You're the nice sister, remember? I'm the wild one who eloped when I was seventeen and regretted it three weeks later. I gave our poor preacher father ulcers until the day he died. I would change that if I could. I'm the storm and you're the port. You're the sensible one. And what you're thinking about doing doesn't make sense."

April couldn't explain it, but she'd seen something in Cole's eyes yesterday, or more accurately, she saw something missing. She'd recognized the emptiness, for she saw the same lost look in her own reflection every day.

"Be careful, April."

"I'm always careful."

"Stubborn and careful are not the same thing. Give it a week. If you still feel it's worth pursuing, you can consider hiring him, or better yet some local builder you've known for years."

"He's coming back tomorrow morning."

"Oh, dear."

April smiled in spite of herself. "Don't worry."

On a groan, Marilee said, "That's what I'm supposed to say when you caution me against doing something I'm going to do anyway. This turnabout is out of my comfort zone."

April laughed softly into the phone.

"What will Jay's family say?" Marilee asked.

April's laughter trailed away. There was a hollow feeling in the pit of her stomach as she thought about the big, bossy, noisy, loving Avery clan, for they'd suffered Jay's loss, too. "They'll be surprised but they'll listen and they'll talk to me and they'll talk to each other and they'll give their opinions and advice. And they'll want to meet the man who was with Jay when he died."

Marilee's sigh matched April's. As if they both felt they'd said enough for one night, they said their usual goodbyes and I love yous before disconnecting. April stood perfectly still, lost in thought for a long time afterward.

Jay's parents owned the busiest real estate company in Orchard Hill. Jim and JoAnn Avery had raised their six children in the same Victorian house they lived in today. The entire family had taken April into the fold the first time Jay brought her home. She considered her sisters-in-law some of her dearest friends. Both of Jay's brothers *happened* to stop by every week. She recognized it as the pretext it was and invariably looked on while they moved something heavy or performed any number of household repairs. She indulged them and they appreciated it, for helping her made them feel closer to Jay.

They mourned him. And missed him. As did she.

It occurred to her, as she finally crawled into bed, fluffed her pillows and turned out the light, that everyone was stuck in the quagmire of missing Jay. And there seemed to be no way out of it.

Behind her closed eyes she pictured her handsome young husband. Jay had had a calm nature and gray eyes that crinkled in the corners, two lines forming between them as he pondered something deep and meaningful.

His mouth had worn a ready smile each day when he returned home from work as an architect with a firm in Grand Rapids, his blond hair windblown from driving with the windows down, his very presence making her and the girls feel safe and cherished.

She imagined him discussing claw-foot bathtubs and walk-in closets with his fellow soldiers to pass the long nights far from home. And she imagined Cole Cavanaugh weighing in on the subject in a bunker thousands of miles away.

In her mind she pictured Cole as he'd been when she'd first seen him on her front stoop yesterday. She'd known he was a soldier instantly, for bravery had its own stance, feet together, shoulders squared, chin up and gaze steady.

She'd recognized him instantly from the photo she'd seen of him standing with Jay in front of a tank in the desert. It had taken only a few more seconds to feel as if she knew him. She hadn't been prepared for that, any more than she'd been ready to let someone finish what Jay hadn't been able to start.

She didn't think Cole Cavanaugh was ready, either, emotionally at least. And yet he'd come here. He'd shared his last memories of Jay, although doing so had drained him, emptying him of something vital, the way burning that mattress had emptied her.

For some reason, Cole needed to be here while he figured out his next step. April couldn't help wondering if perhaps she needed the same thing.

Violet and Gracie Avery were eating breakfast when Cole followed April into her kitchen at eight o'clock sharp Friday morning. It had been three days since he'd first knocked on her door. Technically that wasn't a long time.

He'd thought today would never come.

After leaving here the other day, he'd driven through Orchard Hill on streets named for presidents and trees. He'd crossed the bridge over the Acorn River and discovered Orchard University and the trendy new subdivisions surrounding it. Back on this side of the river, he'd meandered through historic neighborhoods with their stately old homes and large lawns. He'd used up half a tank of gas and burned through an hour before he came upon what he'd been looking for.

He sat at the entrance of Rest in Peace Cemetery for a long time. One day he would drive through the open gate, but on Tuesday he'd circled back to Orchard Road and checked into a room at the Stone Inn.

According to a feisty old redhead who'd flirted outrageously with him and apparently with every other male who checked in, the place was haunted. For the past three nights he'd found himself listening for creaking rocking chairs and squeaky door hinges—anything to pass the time. The thought of specters didn't frighten him, but the sensation that time was standing still had him climbing the walls.

It had been a matter of days since he'd made his initial pitch to April regarding her upstairs, days that had dragged, just like every day dragged. But time hadn't stood still. It was finally Friday. He was here, and so was the moment of truth when he supplied April with an official quote and she either agreed to let him do this or told him no.

The girls were still in their pajamas, Violet's legs wound around the spindly legs of her chair while

Grace's bare feet swung in circles twelve inches off the floor. Looking as fresh as morning dew, their mother wore shorts, a pink sleeveless shirt and sandals with cork wedge heels.

He had a sheaf of papers in his hand. The floor plan was on top, pictures and sketches and blueprints of his most prized projects came next. There were four emailed letters of reference on the bottom, and a dozen more names, phone numbers and email addresses on the last page.

The girls had stopped eating their cereal, and all three of the Avery women were looking at him. "I need to measure the upstairs before I put the final touches on my bid."

"Go ahead," she said. "Why don't you leave everything you have with me in the meantime?"

He handed April the papers then slipped from the room and went upstairs. He measured twice, jotted notes and opened his laptop. He filled in the blanks, computed materials and construction costs, double-checked his figures and the design, then returned to the kitchen where the girls were now eating toast. April was still reading.

"I can go back to the inn and print out a final copy, or email you the finished quote," he said.

"It's finished then?"

She looked at him, and he swore something passed from her gaze to his. "It's all done," he said.

"Can you email it to me right now?" She gave him her address, and with a click of a few buttons, he was done. Instantly her phone chirruped, signaling an incoming email.

He should go. Give her time to look it over. She

would get back to him when she was ready. And yet his feet were rooted to the floor.

It occurred to him that the twins must have said something. He tried to answer, but evidently more was expected of him, because Gracie and Violet didn't resume eating.

"What's for breakfast?" he asked for lack of other ideas.

"Cereal and toast and juice and milk," Gracie replied.

"Want some?" Grace asked, her bread poised in midair over her plate.

"No, thanks." And then, because they continued to look expectantly at him, he added, "I ate breakfast before I drove over."

He glanced at April and saw that she was now looking at her laptop. It would probably take her a while to peruse everything, since he'd included suggestions for wood flooring and shower tiles and bathtubs and fixtures.

"I'll see myself out."

Without looking up, she said, "You're welcome to wait."

The back door was open and the faint sound of birdsong carried inside on this warm, dewy August morning. It wasn't enough to cover the ticking of a nearby clock or the unconscious thrum of his fingers on his jean-clad thigh.

When one of the girls invited him outside to see their playhouse and her twin took up the chorus, April smiled up at him. Cole found himself taking in the glimmer of her eyes. The tenderness in her smile snuck up on him, curling into his chest, settling lower.

Oh, no it didn't. There would be none of that. It woke him up, and pried the soles of his shoes from the floor.

He allowed the kids to draw him to the backyard where he duly praised their playhouse, their swing set, their wading pool and their bicycles complete with training wheels and horns, which they demonstrated. He glanced back at the house once and saw that April now stood at the door where she could keep an eye on her daughters. It humbled him. People called him a hero, but good parents were the true heroes, good single parents especially.

He'd never realized kids talked so much. These two didn't seem to mind that he gave them yes and no answers. They were fascinated by a blue feather they found and the dew on the grass and the tracks their wet feet made on the stone as he followed them back into the house.

Cole stayed just inside the door while Grace and Violet skipped to their room to play.

April had returned to her earlier post across the room. He waited. The clock ticked. His fingers strummed.

Clearing his throat, he said, "My cell number and contact information are on the letterhead. I'll see myself out."

She held up one finger for him to wait.

He found his gaze trained on her. Her waist was narrow, her hips slightly flared. She wore her light brown hair up today. It was secured high on her head with a shiny silver clasp. Tendrils had escaped, curling down her neck and around her ears.

"When can you begin?" she asked.

He started, and silently cursed his shot nerves. Just like that, she was hiring him?

He knew he should answer, *First thing Monday morning.* Or *tomorrow.* Or better yet *today.* His hand went to his forehead, and slowly dragged down his face. "Uh," he said instead.

Brilliant.

She neatened the sheaf of papers by tapping the bottom edges on the counter. Laying all but the last two pages of the bundle down, she looked at him again.

"I included the phone numbers of each of my references," he said. "You should call them."

"Amelia Bradley gave your work ethic—and, I quote, 'your boyish shyness'—five stars."

He started. Amelia Bradley was a grandmother of seven who'd tried to fatten him up the entire time Cavanaugh & Maloney had been rebuilding her home after a fire. "You've really already called Mrs. Bradley?"

"While you were outside with the girls. She wants you to know she's doing well and she says hello. She also said there is no finer builder than you."

Cole was at a loss. "What about the other references? Are you planning to check them?"

"Are you planning to leave the job half-finished?"

"Of course not."

"Do shoddy work?"

He shook his head.

"Begin before 8:00 a.m.?" she asked.

This time he held perfectly still.

"Well?" she prodded.

He was trying to decide if that was a trick question. "Do you want me to begin before eight?"

"Oh, gosh, no."

She smiled. And he felt it sneaking inside him again. "Then I won't begin before eight."

They stared at one another, Cole near the door, April near the refrigerator, a dozen feet separating them. "Is everything all right?" she asked.

With the world, with wars, and pain and suffering and the people whose greed caused both? There was plenty wrong if he looked for it. But right now he was looking at April's mouth. "Why are you smiling?" he asked.

She rested her back against the cabinet behind her, crossed her ankles and folded her arms. Gosh, she was pretty. It would have been easy to stare, in fact it was damn close to impossible not to, but he forced his gaze to hers and kept it there.

"Maybe I'm smiling because I think you need it," she replied. "The same way you need this job."

"I'm not some charity case, April."

"I've noticed," she said.

Cole was staring into her eyes, and April wondered where he'd learned to hold so still. So far he'd been the epitome of professional thoroughness. He was a successful builder with a construction company of his own out East. And yet he was here. At 404 Baldwin Street. In Orchard Hill, Michigan.

"For the record, I'm not a charity case, either. This isn't about money, is it?"

He shook his head.

It was about Jay. He didn't say it. Neither of them did, but they both knew it was true.

When he thanked her for her time and started back through the living room the way he'd come, she followed him. "I'll see you on Monday," she said.

"Monday," he agreed. "But not before eight."

She felt herself smile all over again. "Cole?"

He looked back at her from the stoop.

"The front door is for company and guests. The side door is for friends and family. Use that one next time, okay?"

He nodded, and it was settled. He left then. Watching him through the screen, she noticed he relied heavily on the railing to descend the steps, but he didn't limp as he continued on toward his black Ford. He climbed in and closed his door before he looked back at her. Her wave was a brief flutter of her hand. His was more of a salute before he drove away.

Breathless, she returned to her sunny kitchen and read over the remaining two pages of references Cole had given her. Reaching the end, she realized she couldn't recall a single word she'd read.

The girls were playing happily in their room. Normally their voices had a calming effect on her.

Putting the papers with the others in the stack, she closed her email then placed her fingertips over the thrumming pulse at the base of her neck. Her breathing was shallow and her heart beat too fast. She was scared to death, and she knew why.

She'd noticed Cole.

Not as a former soldier who favored his right leg slightly on stairs. Not as a carpenter here to finish what his best friend couldn't begin.

But as a man.

It was one thing to notice his scent. That was as natural to her as breathing. But how could she have memorized every nuance in his lean face—how his cheeks were slightly hollowed, his jaw firm, his neck, shoulders, chest, hips and thighs like corded bronze?

She'd noticed his hands, too. They were broad across the knuckles and slightly scuffed up, so unlike Jay's. She remembered the way Cole stood, feet slightly apart, shoulders broad, gaze steady. And remembering all those parts of him, she felt—

Something.

A pull, a small tug on her insides.

Her hands went to her hot face. She didn't want to feel this way, but there it was, a stirring low in her belly.

Jay, where are you? she silently cried.

The only reply was the sigh of the wind. And she felt bereft all over again.

Breathing deeply, she placed her hands over her heart. Eyes closed, she felt her love for her husband there.

She was still in love with Jay. She found comfort in that.

Cole Cavanaugh had his wounds and his demons. Some people called it baggage. And April had hers. They were both stubborn, each of them determined not to take charity. They each needed something from the other. Not closure—Lord, no, she had issues with that word. Certainly not sex. Whatever it was they needed, they would figure it out without that.

The trouble was, Jay was gone and Cole was here. Jay was dead. And she wasn't.

Standing there, one hand on her warm cheek and the other covering her racing heart, she was definitely not dead. In fact, she hadn't felt alive in this way in a long time. Fourteen months and six days to be exact. And it scared the daylights out of her.

Placing the neatened stack of papers on top of the microwave, she slowly turned around. The girls' breakfast dishes were still on the table and their chairs still pushed out. She took in the dripping faucet, the sun slanting through the window above it. There was Gracie's and Violet's artwork on the fridge and a hair tie on the counter, April's sunglasses on the shelf near the door and her cell phone on the charger. Nothing had changed since last week or the week before that. That little twinge had been an aberration. End of story.

With that, she gathered used cups, cereal bowls and spoons, wiped the spilled milk from the table and continued on with the ordinary business of her day.

Other than the faint creak of the floor beneath the soles of his shoes, all was quiet in the Stone Inn when Cole emerged from his room shortly before ten on Saturday morning. Nobody had been up when he'd crept out for coffee at daybreak, either. He was hoping his luck continued.

The inn had been built more than one hundred years ago for a wealthy family whose last name was Stone. If Cole had been in charge of the renovations, he would have done a few things differently, but all in all the elegant charm of the former mansion had been preserved and every modern luxury and amenity added. The bed-and-breakfast inn had central air, spacious rooms with private baths, comfortable overstuffed chairs and beds all decked out in luxurious cotton sheets, locally made quilts and half a dozen pillows.

He wasn't sorry he'd chosen this place. Now, if he could make it to the parking lot without being waylaid, he would consider himself a lucky man.

Carrying his laptop beneath one arm, he listened intently as he rounded the corner in the upstairs hallway. All was quiet on this floor. So far, so good.

Painstakingly descending the open staircase, he noticed the lingering aroma of strong coffee and bacon and maple syrup, but the dining room was empty and the front desk was vacant. Ten more steps and he would be out the door.

He'd taken three when someone called, "There you are! I almost missed you."

So close. His exit thwarted, Cole refrained from groaning, and carefully did a one-eighty.

The redhead who covered the front desk when the innkeeper was out was sauntering toward him. Dressed all in purple again today, Harriet Ferris batted fake eyelashes behind her trifocals and said, "This is my sashay. Feel free to admire it."

He smiled in spite of himself.

Seventy-five if she was a day, the audacious bodacious woman stood five feet two in her three-inch heels. She may have been small, but her personality made her impossible to ignore.

Peering up at him myopically, she said, "My goodness, but I like a man who doesn't overuse his comehither smile. Just between you and me, my Walter is in for some serious competition, if you play your cards right, that is. Where are you sneaking off to at this time of the morning, anyway?"

"What makes you think I was sneaking?"

She made a dismissive sound between her pursed lips. "I'm a good listener, you know, but you aren't going to stay and talk to me, are you?"

"It isn't that I don't enjoy talking to people, pretty redheads, especially."

Harriet raised one penciled-on eyebrow. She may have been an outrageous flirt, but she was no dummy. "Your leg is bothering you again today, isn't it?" she asked.

He couldn't help it if his eyes widened.

Waving her hand as if at a bothersome fly, she said, "You used your real name and I'm good with a computer. It's like I always say, it's the quiet ones you want to watch. Although it pains me to say this, your secret is safe with me. Still, I wish you would allow Summer's husband to write an exclusive about you. People would come from miles around to thank you for your sacrifices for our country if they knew."

Cole shook his head. Summer Merrick's husband owned and operated the local newspaper, and Cole didn't want strangers stopping him on the street to shake his hand. He wasn't here for glory. "I prefer to keep a low profile."

Harriet sighed dramatically. "First our resident ghost decides to lay low." She shook her head dramatically, and Cole recalled hearing of a ghost that supposedly resided here in the old inn. "And now I have a decorated war hero in my midst and I can't even tell anybody. Go if you must, but be careful if you're driving anywhere today. This humidity brings out the crazy in people." With a wink, she added, "There's nothing like it to get the juices flowing, though, if you know what I mean."

"Something tells me people always know what you mean, Harriet."

"Scoff if you want, but when the temperature and humidity climb, clothes come off. Consider yourself duly warned."

"I'll take it under advisement, Harriet."

Fanning herself with one hand, she said, "With that swagger and those eyes, women must be lining up."

He walked out the door without commenting because he didn't want women lining up. There was only one woman he wanted. There. He'd admitted it, to himself at least. He waited for the sky to open up or the earth to begin to shake.

It would be bad enough if he'd started wanting her after Jay died. But Cole had dreamed of April before. Logically, he knew a man couldn't control his dreams, but he still felt guilty as hell about it.

He could, and would control himself in every other way. Because he didn't see how he would live with himself if he didn't. And Cole couldn't explain it, but for the first time since Jay had died, Cole felt alive, as if until now he'd just been going through the motions. He was alive. For the first time in a long time, he was almost glad about that.

Chapter Three

Although the temperature and humidity continued to climb, contrary to Harriet Ferris's prediction, the only ill temper Cole encountered during his drive to April's house came from a honeybee that flew in the open passenger window and got desperate when it couldn't find its way out. Cole reached April's driveway in record time, shoved the shift lever into Park and dove out of the truck, the bee right behind him.

One hand on his thigh, he straightened from his crouch and looked around to see if anybody had witnessed his ungainly landing. April's garage doors were open and two cars were inside. Somebody in the neighborhood was playing music the way he used to when he was a teenager washing his first car. Two small bicycles sat in the driveway, their riders nowhere in sight.

In a yard behind April's, a sprinkler oscillated, the

spray visible above an aging privacy hedge. Bits of colorful swimsuits appeared through the sparse foliage as screeching children darted through the spray.

After retrieving his laptop from the passenger seat, Cole stepped over a pair of flowered garden gloves lying on top of a small pile of weeds on the sidewalk. He started toward the front door before he recalled April's invitation to use the side door from now on. Going to that one instead, he knocked briskly on the sturdy screen.

"Somebody's here, April." It was a man's voice. And it came from inside.

She was at the door within seconds. "Cole. Hello." Did she sound breathless?

He hadn't considered the possibility that she might be seeing someone. "I should have called," he said, stifling the urge to shuffle from foot to foot. "I didn't see a car, but if you're busy I'll come back another time."

"Don't be silly. Come in."

"You have company."

But she didn't listen. Opening the door for him, she smiled and said, "Days like this make me wonder why I don't have central air. What this humidity does to my hair alone is reason enough."

It didn't seem to matter that he didn't comment. She led him past a small laundry room and closet. Her hair looked good to him, soft, touchable and resilient. Like the rest of her. She wore blue shorts today and a sleeveless shirt with buttons down the back. She looked sexy and dewy, and damn, he really should have called instead of stopping in unannounced. A decision about the windows upstairs could have waited, but it was too late now.

In the kitchen a man was running water at April's sink. Wearing a T-shirt and running shorts, he was fit and tan and seemed to know his way around her place.

"Will, this is Cole Cavanaugh. He—"

"Cole Cavanaugh," the guy repeated, interrupting her. "Jay's best friend in the army?"

Cole was pretty sure the reverence in the other man's voice was genuine. Obviously he'd known Jay well, and he knew April, too, well enough in fact to complete her sentences.

The breeze from an oscillating fan fluttered her curly hair, its low hum blending with outdoor music and the occasional shrieks of children at play. "As I told April," Cole said tersely, "if this is a bad time, I'll come back later."

"I can't speak for April but it's not a bad time for me," the other man said. "I just finished fixing her leaky faucet."

Backing up a step, Cole turned to April. "I tried to buy new windows for the upstairs, but there's a problem with the sizes. I can order them if you want, but it'll take four weeks for them to come in. I have a few alternatives for you to look at. Online." He held up his laptop. "I'll just show them to you Monday morning. After eight."

April eyed him oddly before turning to Will-who-ever-the-hell-he-was. "I've decided to use some of the money from your great-aunt Lucille's trust fund to finish the upstairs."

"Technically she wasn't our great-aunt," Will said patiently.

Cole wanted to call him out for correcting April. Who did he think he was?

"She was my grandmother's closest friend. She had no family, so she adopted the Avery clan." The other man turned his hands up and shrugged one shoulder.

There was something familiar about the gesture. "Will," Cole said with a dawning realization. "As in William. You're Jay's brother Billie?"

The guy grimaced. "Jay dubbed me Billie when I was two years old. He's the only one who never outgrew it."

This was one of Jay's brothers. His younger brother. Cole saw it now, the likeness through the eyes, the lanky build and wry humor. It was good Cole hadn't flattened him.

"He called *me* C.C.," he said as he accepted Will Avery's handshake.

Will's grip was strong, and in it he conveyed the strength of what he was feeling. Cole accepted the handshake but was relieved the younger man didn't voice his thoughts out loud.

"Are you a plumber?" Cole asked since it seemed to him that the silence called for conversation.

Will Avery put a wrench in a small toolbox and put the toolbox under April's sink before he said, "I'm a passing do-it-yourselfer at best. All the more reason to have enormous respect for tradesmen's abilities."

April's voice startled both men. "Will teaches English literature at our local high school. He and Kristy and their three little boys live behind us, one yard over. The girls are playing there this morning."

Cole felt April's smile clear to his knees. "So that's who's making all the racket back there," he said.

She nodded.

"And that explains why there isn't an extra car in your driveway. He walked over."

"What did you think?" she asked.

"Never mind."

Her smile only broadened. "Both of Jay's brothers keep this place from falling down around the girls and me. Will was also enormously instrumental in helping me get back into teaching. Nobody writes a letter of recommendation quite like an English literature teacher."

"I didn't know you were a teacher," Cole said to her.

"Fifth grade. I was a teacher when I met Jay, but I've been out of the classroom since the girls were born. I'm starting back at our local elementary school this fall."

Cole was aware she'd been a homemaker, but he'd never asked Jay what she'd done before that. It made him realize there was a great deal about her he didn't know.

"I'd planned to stay home until the twins were a little older," she continued. "But then—"

They both felt what she'd left unsaid.

Jay's brother cleared his throat. Oh. That's right. They weren't alone.

"I need to get going, April," Will said. "The new baby is a dream but I'm sure Kristy could use a break." He held the front of his shirt away from his body. "I think I'll hit the sprinkler on my way through my backyard. Thank God we have air-conditioning. It was good to meet you, Cole. I mean that."

"You, too," Cole said.

"Would you send Gracie and Violet home?" April asked after thanking her brother-in-law for his help.

When Will was gone, April said, "I've been thinking about the project."

"That's why I'm here." He reached down and opened his laptop on the table as she came up next to him.

"Cole, what happened?" She gently laid her fingertips next to the welt on the back of his neck.

"Just a little bee sting." He straightened, causing her hand to land on his shoulder.

He didn't know how long they stood that way, her hand resting lightly on the breadth of his right shoulder while his hands remained at his sides, itching to touch her. Why did she have to be beautiful?

"A bee stung you?" she asked. "I hope you're not allergic." As she spoke, his gaze was naturally drawn to her mouth. Pretty, it was bow-shaped, her bottom lip fuller than the top. So kissable.

He tore his gaze away and eased backward. "I'm not allergic," he said. "And it wasn't the bee's fault."

She went to a cabinet near the sink and reached to an upper shelf. For a moment, her stretch bared a patch of skin at her waist. Cole wasn't a prisoner to his hormones, but it sure wasn't easy to look away.

Taking out a tube of ointment, she returned to the table and pulled out a chair. "Have a seat," she said. "This medicine works miracles on bee stings. It'll relieve the itch and burn, guaranteed."

He reached for the ointment, but she was already squeezing a small amount onto her finger. Eyeing the chair she held, Cole wavered, but in the end he did as she instructed. From behind him, she drew the collar of his shirt away from the welt. Her touch indescribably soft, she gently applied the ointment in a circular motion.

"It shouldn't take long to begin working," she said, dabbing on more cream.

His head listed forward of its own accord. His breathing deepened as he relaxed, her fingertips working the cream into the sting that already seemed to burn less. He imagined those fingers gliding along the top of his collar, perhaps skimming the side of his jaw before coming to rest at the base of his throat. From there he imagined them moving languidly down the center of his chest, pausing briefly, moving again.

"Where were you when you got stung?" Her question brought his head up.

He heard a wrapper of some sort being torn close to his ear. "Somewhere between Division Street and Elm. The bee probably thought he'd take a quick shortcut through the cab of my truck on his way to the flowers across the street. The light was turning green and I didn't notice him until I'd already started through the intersection. Apparently he didn't appreciate being shanghaied."

"I see." She applied a Band-Aid and drew his collar over it, her touch so light it was almost as if she'd followed up with a kiss. The notion made him ache.

He fought it with everything he had. She was Jay's widow. He was here to find peace and hopefully bring her a little, too. Nothing more.

Finished with her ministering, she recapped the tube and returned it to the cabinet. This time, he didn't watch.

Before he heard the cupboard door close with a quiet thud, Cole got to his feet and pushed his chair back in where it belonged. "Would you like to take a look at other windows?" he asked.

"About that," she said. "I'm sorry for wasting your time."

He braced for imminent bad news. She must have guessed what he'd been imagining, and decided against letting him do her remodel. He wouldn't blame her, but eyeing her guardedly, he waited for her to confirm it.

"I'm considering making some changes to your design," she said.

That was all? Relief washed over him. Every remodel went through changes, especially in the beginning. "It's Jay's design, but by all means," he said. "This is your home and your decision, and I want you to be absolutely happy with the renovations. What would you like changed?"

"We're home, Mama!" The door slammed and Gracie bounded into the kitchen, dripping wet, dragging her beach towel behind her. The door slammed a second time and Violet followed her sister inside, also dripping, her towel wadded into a ball beneath her arm.

"Uncle Will turned the sprinkler off and said we had to come home," Violet said.

"We didn't wanna, but then he told Aunt Kristy Cole was here," Gracie explained. "So we ran all the way."

Violet looked up at him. "Wanna watch us ride our bikes without the training wheels? We just learned how last night."

"Girls, he can watch you ride your bikes another time. You're leaving puddles." While the twins looked down with shock and dismay so genuine it was comical, their mother dried them both with Violet's towel and wiped the floor with Grace's.

These two looked more alike than Cole had first thought. They wore one-piece swimsuits; Gracie's was green, Violet's was yellow, both had ruffles around the legs and bows on the straps. Wet, Violet's curly hair was almost straight and Gracie's blond hair appeared darker, more like her sister's. They had similar noses and chins, knobby knees and narrow feet, which currently had blades of grass stuck to them.

How many times had Jay told him they took his breath away? Cole would never forget the wonder and the ache in Jay's voice when he spoke of them.

April instructed her daughters to change into dry clothes. "Is Cole staying for lunch, Mama?" Gracie asked.

Three pairs of eyes were on him suddenly.

"I'll ask him," April said, pointing firmly at the doorway leading to the hall. And the girls ran to do as they were told.

Cole shook his head lest she voice the invitation. "About those changes," he said instead.

"Could we go over them another time?"

"Ah. Sure. Of course. No problem." He clamped his mouth shut before things got worse.

"It isn't that I'm not interested in discussing them with you. It's just that I'm having a cookout tonight," she explained. "It's in the early planning stages," she told him, her chin lowering in a conniving manner.

"How early?" he heard himself ask.

"I just decided this minute. And you should join us."

"I—that is, I don't, I mean…" Forfeiting his idiotic stammering, he stopped shuffling backward and held still.

"What I meant to say is, we would be honored if you would join us, Cole."

He could hear the girls talking as they slammed drawers, and he knew he didn't have long to let their mother down gently.

"It's come as you are," April continued, the fan whirring on the counter behind her, fluttering the curls around her shoulders. "We're a very low-key bunch, dress code-wise."

"We who?" he asked.

"I won't have an exact head count until after I actually start inviting everyone. It'll be the girls and me for sure, Jay's brother Ben, his wife, Gabby, and their daughter, and Will, Kristy and their boys. I'll also invite Jay's parents, two of his sisters and their husbands and kids, and a few friends and my next-door neighbors, if they're not busy."

He was shaking his head long before she'd finished.

Growing up an only child, Cole steered clear of large families and noisy crowds. There were too many undercurrents and too much past and way too many nuances. He preferred small groups. And besides, this was Jay's family.

Not Cole's.

He'd been recovering from a serious infection in the wound in his side in a hospital stateside the day they'd buried Jay, so Cole had been unable to attend the funeral. Now, he tried to recall what his friend had told him about his parents and siblings. It seemed there were two brothers, three sisters, half a dozen in-laws and several nieces and nephews. Jay's descriptions had blurred in Cole's mind, and he'd never tried to keep them straight.

"I'm really not much for crowds, April."

"You mean, since—"

"No. I mean, yes, more so now, but I've never enjoyed crowds." It was true. Cole had been an only child, and had no first cousins. He had a few friends at school, but until college he was content for the most part to talk to adults or be alone. He'd dated, thought he was in love a few times, but those relationships hadn't lasted. He used to be on a softball team, played a little racquetball, but by then he was working day and night to get the business off the ground and fitting the National Guard into his schedule, and being alone didn't feel lonely. Nobody was more surprised than he was when he and Jay struck a chord the first time they met.

She leaned her back against the counter again and crossed her arms as she had the last time he was here. Now he knew the stance wasn't as innocent as it appeared. Any second now she was going to attempt to change his mind.

"You heard Gracie," she said. "Will told Kristy you're here. By now, she's called Gabby, and they've probably both texted Beth and Regan. Word's out you're in Orchard Hill. You can either meet them all, all at once, or you can wait for them to stop by individually to get a good look at you."

He stared at her incredulously. "Those are my only two options?"

Her melodious laugh snuck into his chest.

"Trust me, they'll come because you're a link to Jay. The fact that you're going to be renovating my upstairs sweetens the honeypot."

Cole was glad that damn bee hadn't followed him into the house because he was pretty sure his mouth was gaping.

"Don't worry," April continued. "They're good people. They'd give anyone in need the shirt off their backs. Okay, maybe they're a little bossy. They all have strong opinions and will probably share them with you in regard to the upstairs. On a slow night they'll discuss politics with you, and gas prices, religion and the weather.

"If you don't attend the impromptu gathering tonight I guarantee they'll find some reason to stop over one at a time while you're trying to work on the upstairs. I've found it's better to get things like this over with in one fell swoop."

He didn't know what to say.

"You look stupefied." She made a wry face. "Now there's a word you don't hear every day," April said.

He didn't even try to smile. "I'm trying to keep a low profile while I'm here."

"You're about to discover that's impossible." She held his gaze but it wasn't enough to sway him to promise to come over later. Before he had the chance to say he *wouldn't* attend, she said, "I hope you join us, but attendance isn't mandatory. I'll put you down for a maybe."

End of discussion. The woman was good.

He waited to say goodbye until the girls had rejoined their mother in the kitchen. Although their forlorn faces were hard to resist, their pleas didn't persuade him to stay for lunch, either. He left before he changed his mind.

Once outside, he took a deep breath. He'd known, in the furthest recesses of his mind, that finishing Jay's upstairs would test his reclusive tendencies. The idea of meeting the Averys all at once brought back his last dreams, the ones he'd had before Jay died.

In the first dream Cole and Jay had been flying. There was no magic carpet or arms flapping. They were simply soaring high above the earth, darting faster and faster. Behind them dark shadows like bloodhounds hunted them, coming so close Cole felt their hot breath on the back of his neck. Suddenly the rest of their unit was there, too. There was a deafening explosion. Yelling. Chaos. One minute Jay was beside him. The next he was gone.

Cole had awakened in a cold sweat.

He'd always been a lucid dreamer. It was common among soldiers to dream of death. Under the circumstances, dreaming of flying wasn't a stretch, either. It had other connotations, but escape was inherent among them.

He'd had dreams of explosions before. Once, his unit had orders to secure an abandoned building that according to intel had been headquarters for a band of terrorists. The night before the mission Cole had dreamed that he and five men entered a building where a massive IED immediately detonated. The following day, Cole and his men didn't enter that building until bomb specialists had neutralized a deadly IED.

Cole didn't always dream before an attack. In fact, more often than not, he didn't dream at all, but when he did, he paid attention. The dreams about Jay and him flying had left Cole feeling unsettled, a knife in the pit of his stomach.

Two days later their unit was ambushed. There was a deafening explosion. Yelling. Chaos. Men screaming in pain. Cole and Jay were thrown like rag dolls twenty feet backward. Wounded, Cole crept to where Jay lay on the hot sand, alive but barely. They bled together, and despite Cole's orders for Jay to hold on until help arrived, they both knew that wasn't possible.

When Jay took his last breath, Cole wept. He'd stayed with his friend, his war brother, one bloodied hand on Jay's still chest, until they were lifted onto gurneys. Jay began his final journey home and Cole was taken to a hospital where he would undergo surgery to remove the shrapnel from his side.

When his injury healed he'd returned to combat until his second injury, one that nearly took his leg and his life. He hadn't dreamed again. Not once. He'd thought about his dreams, though, all of them, that last one especially. More than anything, he recalled all the stories Jay had told about home. Somehow those tender, humorous depictions of his best friend's family sustained Cole through bleak days, indescribable pain and grueling physical therapy. It was as if Jay's words had introduced Cole to April.

Cole supposed he'd fallen a little in love with her while listening to the cadence of Jay's deep voice painting pictures of their life in Orchard Hill, Michigan. Although he wasn't proud of it, it was harmless then. During his difficult recovery, those stories brought Cole solace, somehow. But as the weeks turned into months, he started to think about meeting her, just meeting her. Nothing more.

And now he had.

He didn't steal or cheat and he couldn't tell a lie to save his own skin. He wasn't a jealous man. He'd never begrudged his best friend his happiness. They'd been joined at the hip, the guys in their unit had often said. He wasn't about to try to insinuate himself into Jay's family, certainly not into April's life.

Cole would never attempt to take Jay's place. And that was final.

"Think he'll come tonight, Mama?"

Violet and Gracie gazed wistfully out the screen door Cole had just exited. April knew he'd driven away when they left their post.

Would he join them this evening?

She wasn't sure what to make of his hasty retreat. Holding her right hand in her left, she didn't know what to make of the tingling sensation in her fingertips, either.

She held them to her cheek as lightly as she'd skimmed them over the welt on Cole's neck. Doing so brought back the acceleration of her heart rate and the guilt that immediately followed.

It wasn't as if anything would come of a few tingles in her fingertips and flutters in her heart. She liked Cole Cavanaugh. She liked most people, but she liked him especially. She didn't know him well, but it didn't matter. Something inside him called to her, and she wasn't sorry he was here.

Did she think he would join the gathering tonight to meet Jay's family? Good question. She hoped he would. She hadn't been exaggerating about her in-laws. They were wonderful people and they would meet him, one way or another.

Now she had a barbecue to plan. She began by sending out a mass text inviting the Averys, her neighbors and a few close friends to her house later today. It was short notice, but it was summer, and she knew the people closest to her. They'd always been a tight-knit group. Losing Jay had made them cling tighter to one another. For them, any reason was a good reason to get together. And they would move heaven and earth if it meant they might meet the man who'd shared the last months with Jay.

Taking out a loaf of bread, she began preparing egg salad sandwiches for lunch. She quartered them diagonally and added chips and blueberries to three plates. It wasn't long before the answering texts began coming in.

Of course we'll come! her sister-in-law, Kristy texted. I just made a bowl of potato salad. I'll bring it along.

Sounds like fun, her best friend, Lacey Sullivan, who was expecting twins, replied. Put me down for brownies with cream cheese and real fudge.

Maddie has a friend over, April's sister-in-law Gabby wrote. Is it okay if she comes, too?

For the next hour, texts were exchanged, April's menu was discussed and side dishes were evaluated, with some scratched off the list and new ones substituted. Jay's family would swoop in the way they always did, big and loving and boisterous and accepting. She didn't know how she would have gotten through the past fourteen months without them.

Her own father had been a wonderful preacher. Sadly he'd died too young. Like April, her mother had always been strong and independent. Right now she was in Africa with her church group building a school for orphans. Though every bit as caring, her family had never been as loud and bossy as Jay's, and yet April had quickly acclimated to their enthusiasm. Surely Cole could handle it for one night.

But would he come?

After lunch she and the girls went to the grocery store for charcoal and all the fixings for a barbecue. She spruced up the house and set out the paper plates and plastic cutlery. She was deciding on drinks when one final text came in. It was from Jay's mother and spoke for them all.

Is Cole Cavanaugh what you expected?

Was he? April took a shower and gave Gracie and Violet a bath. Helping the girls into sundresses, she sighed.

Other than offering up a silent prayer for his recovery a year ago, she hadn't considered what Cole Cavanaugh was like. She certainly hadn't expected him to appear on her doorstep. She didn't know what to expect this evening, either.

She remembered how he'd looked at her when she'd first touched his bee sting. For the span of two heartbeats, they'd stood but a hairbreadth apart, and she'd done it again: she'd breathed him in. He was crisp new snow on the hottest day of the year.

His muscles had tensed and every inch of him had gone on red alert. Was he uncomfortable with the slightest human touch or was he starving for it?

His eyes had widened when she'd told him he needed to join them tonight. Then the shutters had come down.

Would he stop by?

Honestly, she just didn't know. She wanted him to, wanted to see him again. As a friend, she told herself. She prayed that was all it was, because she wasn't ready for this to be anything else. She doubted she would ever be ready.

The tug she felt deep in her belly begged to differ. And she didn't know what she was going to do about it.

Cole parked his truck in the shade along the edge of the paved path that wound through a rolling tract of land on the south end of Orchard Hill. Donning sunglasses, he set off on foot, heading for the area where the trees hadn't had time to grow old.

Other people were visiting today, too, but not many. Cole was aware of them the same way he was aware of the bird that flew across his path and the names on the markers he passed.

He walked up and down rows, back and forth beneath the pummeling sunshine. Finally, he came upon what he was looking for from the back. The first thing he noticed was the dainty handprints etched into the stone. Between them the words *We love you, Daddy.*

At the very top block letters spelled *AVERY.*

Cole's shirt was stuck to the middle of his back from the summer heat. Carefully skirting around to the other side of the marker, he stood statue-still on the soft grass, his eyes on the shiny slab of granite that marked the place where Jay's body now lay.

Jason Matthew Avery

A man of immeasurable honor…
Husband, father, son, brother, friend

May 28, 1986—June 2, 2018

US Army insignia were etched into one corner bearing the stripes that corresponded to Jay's rank as sergeant, along with a perfect replica of his medal of valor. Above that was a quote from the bible.

"Blessed are they that mourn for they shall be comforted."
Matthew 5:4

The words were simple but profound. Standing at attention, Cole breathed deeply, staring at the stone until Jay's name blurred and his face took form in his mind.

I'm here, Cole said silently. *In Orchard Hill. You probably already know that. Either April told you, or you can see from where you are.*

He'd heard of people who'd experienced signs from the great beyond. The fact that he experienced no gooseflesh or flickers of light or otherworldly whispers in his ear didn't deter Cole from telling his best friend where he was staying and that he'd been right: Violet's and Gracie's perfection defied description.

While Cole carried on a silent conversation, a squirrel stopped in front of Jay's headstone. Paying his surroundings little attention, Cole told Jay about his gas mileage and shared a funny story about one of the guys from their old unit. He mentioned a medic they both knew and the gains he and their fellow countrymen had made for their ally. He told him how April and the kids were doing, and that other than missing him, they were well.

He talked for so long the squirrel returned, scuttling up a nearby tree, which set off a raucous chirping and squawking from a pair of blue jays that had claimed that branch. Cole ignored the noise, for he was almost ready to say what he'd come here to say.

He wasn't sure where to begin, but Jay knew him well enough to let him ramble. He talked in circles, and ended with a solemn promise, just between the two of them.

Cole had been so focused for so long he hadn't noticed that the sun had stopped scorching his arms and neck and the shards of light reflecting off the rough-cut edges of the stone marker were no longer blinding. He felt it then, not a sign, but a sprinkle that landed on his forehead and slowly rolled down his temple. He glanced all around and then looked up.

Holy—

He whipped his sunglasses off and started to run.

With his eyes fixed on his truck in the distance, he felt the workout deep in his thigh.

Even if he'd been a sprinter, he wouldn't have made it to shelter in time, for the sky opened up, catching him in a driving downpour. He was winded when he reached his vehicle, and soaking wet, as well. His leather seat was wet, too, for he'd left his windows down.

He got in, inserted his key in the ignition and ran the windows up with the press of two buttons. From far in the distance came the rumble of thunder. Another rumble followed, closer this time. Lightning forked in the western sky. But here in this grassy field there was only thunder and warm rain cascading from clouds so low they seemed to touch the earth on all sides.

Cole started his truck and turned the windshield wipers on high. As he followed the winding path back out through the open gate, his radio died and his phone lost its signal. Pulling into the parking lot at the inn, he coasted to a stop in his usual spot, set the parking brake and made a run for the inn's sweeping front porch. Drenched, he went inside where the innkeeper, Summer Merrick, waved aside his apology over leaving wet tracks on the floor.

He ascended the stairs stiffly, unlocked his door and stripped out of his wet clothes. Toweling off, he crawled into the large bed. He drew the sheet over him, and checked his watch before dropping it onto the nightstand next to his useless phone.

He'd been pushing himself to the brink of his endurance for two years, first in the Middle East and then in grueling physical therapy. He was tired. So tired. He hadn't slept well last night, or the night before that, and while he wouldn't go so far as to say he'd found comfort this afternoon, the promise he'd made to Jay had brought him a glimmer of peace.

He lay on his back between scented sheets, the feather pillows beneath his head unbelievably soft, the air artificially cooled, the room already the hazy color of early evening. Lightning struck and thunder shook the ground the inn sat on.

Outside, a storm raged, bending trees and wreaking havoc with anything not battened down. In a large shadowy room in an inn on the outskirts of Orchard Hill, Cole was already sound asleep.

Chapter Four

April had heard of stairways to heaven, but the rays of yellow sunlight shining through invisible breaks in the clouds looked more like grace shining down all around her. Turning right onto Jefferson Street, she waved to the linemen working diligently to restore electricity to the citizens of Orchard Hill. Hopefully she wouldn't encounter any more closed streets during the remaining five blocks to the Stone Inn.

While she'd been planning her barbecue, a storm erupted out of the blue with a clap of thunder that shook the house. She'd been shutting windows against the driving rain when lightning struck so close she'd reeled backward. The lights flashed out while she was whisking the girls to the basement.

They'd huddled on April's lap, Violet's face buried in her mother's shoulder and Gracie's eyes round. When they'd crept back up the stairs twenty minutes later, the soft patter of rain was all that remained of the storm.

Now the air was a comfortable seventy-six degrees and the humidity was back to normal. Although maple leaves littered her yard, the majority of the damage from one end of Orchard Hill to the other was the result of lightning strikes. It was a miracle no one was hurt.

At least no one she knew of.

The electric company estimated that her power wouldn't be restored until midnight tonight, so she'd postponed the barbecue until tomorrow. Cole was the only one she hadn't contacted because there was something wrong with his phone. She and the girls were on their way to the inn to let him know.

"Look at that tree, Mama." Violet's face was pressed close to the window. "How will they get it back in the hole?"

"They won't," Gracie declared from her side of the back seat. "See the roots? They're out of the ground. It's dead."

"God could put it back in," Violet insisted.

"Could He, Mama?"

Pulling into a parking space well away from the fallen sycamore, April wished she had a dollar for every question these two had asked since setting out on this trek. "I have a feeling this old tree is going to be someone's firewood next winter. You may unfasten your seat belts now."

"Is that Cole's black truck, Mama?"

"I believe it is."

"Do you see him?" Violet asked.

"Not yet." With a daughter holding each hand, April spied one man assessing the damage and three others out of harm's way in the side yard. None of them were tall or raw-boned or smolderingly intense. Cole wasn't among those milling about in the courtyard, either.

"Let's go in," Gracie bossed.

April was already opening the heavy oak door.

She'd attended a bridal shower for a friend here a few years ago. The bed-and-breakfast inn was quieter today and all but deserted. The floors were polished mahogany, the foyer large and open, candles flickering in glass-domed wall sconces. Two overstuffed chairs beckoned invitingly from a cozy nook in a sitting room visible through large French doors.

A puzzle had been started on a small table, seemingly forgotten, and board games were stacked on a shelf nearby. The only person in sight was sitting at the innkeeper's desk near the stairs. It wasn't Summer Merrick, the innkeeper herself, but the high-spirited woman who lived next door.

"Hello, Mrs. Ferris. I have a favor to ask."

The diminutive redhead's eyes grew large behind her thick glasses. "Hello, April dear, and a good afternoon to Violet and Gracie, too. If you're hoping to rent a room because your power's out, I'm afraid ours is out, too."

"It's not that," April said. "I wonder if you would deliver a message to one of your guests."

"Which one, dear?"

"Cole Cavanaugh."

There was no reason to suspect the glint in Harriet's faded blue eyes was anything but idle curiosity. "You know Cole?" she asked.

While April was trying to decide how many details she needed to share, Harriet said, "Of course you do. Why else would you wish to have a message delivered to him, hmm? I haven't seen him since this morning. If he's upstairs, he's the only guest who is. The others are outside telling storm stories. Summer is standing in line at the gas station trying to buy ice, and I really shouldn't leave my post at the desk."

"I see."

"Are those suckers?"

"Gracie!" April admonished.

Harriet was already opening the glass jar on the desk. Winking at April, she said, "Why don't you go up and deliver your message while these two and I have a contest to see who can finish our lollipop without biting?"

"I don't want to take advantage of—"

"Nonsense." Harriet popped a sucker into her mouth. "His is room eight." Pointing with an arthritic finger, she said, "Turn right at the top of the stairs, then all the way to the end of the hall."

A woman of indiscernible age, Harriet Ferris had been a fixture in Orchard Hill all her life. She'd taught Jay and two of his sisters Sunday school and had always had a way with people, children and men especially. Mr. Ferris adored her. With Gracie and Violet happily engaged in their contest, April started up the sweeping open staircase.

"Don't you worry about the g-h-o-s-t," Harriet called around her orange lollipop. "No one has seen her for days."

Goose bumps did a rainbow dance along April's arms. A ghost? She believed in grace and eternity and karma and the possibility that somewhere beyond the Milky Way other life might exist.

But a ghost?

April just couldn't see it. Smiling at her own wittiness, she turned right at the top of the stairs, the hem of her light summer dress brushing her knees like a whisper.

The only illumination on this floor came from the faint sunlight spilling through the windows on either end of the narrow hallway. The floors were polished oak, but a carpet runner muted her footsteps.

She reached room eight and paused before the closed door. Turning her head slightly, she listened for some sound from within. The door opened a few inches on silent hinges.

She hadn't touched it. She would swear to it, and yet she found herself looking over her shoulder. The curtain at the end of the hall billowed softly in the slight breeze. She supposed it was possible the wind could have been responsible for opening Cole's door. Why wasn't it latched and locked?

Eyeing the door, ajar now, she listened again. From inside there came a rustle and what sounded like a mattress shifting slightly.

"Cole?" she said softly. "It's me. April."

This time she heard only silence.

She considered returning to the front desk and asking Harriet for a pen and paper to leave a note, but she happened to spy a small table near the door inside Cole's room. On it was a lamp, a pad of pale yellow stationery and a pen. If she could reach that pen and paper, she would jot a quick note.

She called Cole's name again. Hearing no response, she stretched her arm through the narrow opening without stepping over the threshold and found the edge of the table with her fingertips. Reaching a few inches farther, she touched the pen.

It rolled off, onto the floor.

Holding in an impatient huff, she bent down to get it. In the process her shoulder accidentally nudged the door, and it swung open.

She rose from her crouch, the pen in her hand, and saw that the room was large and contained a tall chest of drawers and a high-backed chair. The floor-to-ceiling drapes tinted the air the bronze of early evening. Between the windows was a four-poster bed, and in it, a man, dark-haired and raw-boned, lay covered to his waist.

"Cole?" she called softly.

His eyelashes didn't so much as flutter. After a careful study of his chest, she detected movement, in and out, and in again. He appeared to be sound asleep.

His chest was spattered sparsely with dark hair. His abs were ridged, his navel a shadow, the lower half of him covered loosely with a beige sheet.

A wild fluttering began in her chest and heat flooded her cheeks. For heaven's sake, it wasn't as if she'd never seen a man's bare chest. Before Cole woke up and caught her staring like an imbecile and blushing like a schoolgirl, she tiptoed the remaining few feet to that table. Her back to the room, she quickly jotted a note, all her concentration focused on her task.

"Is Cole dead?"

April's heart nearly exploded. Gracie stood in the doorway, one strap of her light blue sundress sliding off one shoulder. Her lips were purple from her lollipop, wisps of fine blond hair framing her angelic face.

"Gracie, shhh."

"Well, is he?" For an angel, her little girl had a whisper that could penetrate steel.

"No. Now hush," April said quietly. "I'm leaving him a note."

"Is Cole naked?" Of course, Violet was now here, too. She pushed her way inside next to her sister. Her lips were red from her lollipop, her sundress yellow, her curly hair held away from her cherubic face with mismatched barrettes.

"That's rude and it's none of our business."

"He is," Gracie said to her sister.

Holding one hand out to bar her darling daughters from walking right up to the bed to get a better look, she hurriedly signed the note. "When he wakes up and sees this he'll know the barbecue has been postponed until tomorrow. Let's go."

"Wait." Violet planted her feet in front of the table and began to draw a rainbow on the stationery. Communicating in their silent twin-speak, Grace accepted the small square her sister tore off for her. The instant Violet was finished with the pen, Gracie painstakingly began drawing a picture of a house.

April dropped her face into her hands. Slowly spreading her fingers, she chanced a glance at Cole.

His eyes remained closed—thank God—and his chest still rose and fell rhythmically. As far as she could tell, he hadn't stirred.

"There," she whispered the moment Gracie finished, too. "Let's go. Quietly. Cole's tired and we don't want to wake him."

"Why's he tired?"

"I don't know, Violet."

"Why isn't he wearing any pajamas?" Gracie asked.

"I don't know."

"Do we have to wear pajamas tonight?" Violet asked.

"Yes, you do." April practically dragged them out of the room, as they craned their necks to get one last look at the man inside. Pulling the door closed behind them, April fought the desire to sag against the wall in relief.

They met Harriet on their way to the stairs. "There you two are," she said to the girls. And to their mother, "Did you find him?"

"Yes," April answered.

"He's naked," Gracie declared.

Harriet's eyebrows arched tellingly. "Is that so?"

"He's covered and sound asleep." April found she was still whispering.

"He's only covered up with a sheet," Gracie insisted.

"He's naked all right," the girls said in unison, only to begin giggling as if life was richly entertaining.

Harriet winked, and April absolutely positively refused to say one more word on the subject.

While four females of various ages were descending the wide, open staircase in the beautiful old inn on the outskirts of Orchard Hill, Cole opened his eyes. Surfacing as if from the depths of an ocean, he blinked groggily. As the room came into focus, he saw that his phone and watch lay on the bedside table where he'd left them; the bathroom door was ajar, also as he'd left it; and his room door was closed.

Everything appeared to be as it was before he'd fallen into bed, and yet he had the strangest sensation that someone had been here. Maybe there really was a ghost haunting the inn.

From down the hall came the sounds of muffled conversation and giggles. He recognized April's voice, and that twitter had to belong to Harriet, and the gigglers sounded suspiciously like Violet and Gracie.

What were April and the girls doing at the inn? On the second floor, no less?

He went up on one elbow and saw three squares of paper on the table near the door. Something came to him then, a memory not entirely formed. Had someone called his name?

He swung his feet over the side of the bed and sat up. Pulling on yesterday's jeans, he found his feet and limped across the room. He picked up all three sheets of paper. The first was from April, the other two from her little girls. There was no ghost in Cole's room; there was only the ghost of his smile, the first he'd experienced in a long time.

The barbecue was in full swing in April's backyard on Sunday evening. Ben and Will Avery and their wives were playing a beanbag game. Kristy and Gabby were winning, and they were making sure everyone knew it. Several feet away Jim Avery was holding his newest grandson in the crook of his arm, while nearly a dozen other children ran around the yard playing tag and screaming as loud as they could while their mothers grimaced and their fathers pretended they didn't hear. Two of April's neighbors and her mother-in-law were discussing a book they'd read recently.

April glided from one group to the next with beverages, a tray of appetizers and a welcoming smile. Although she didn't say it, she felt the lack of Jay's presence. Everyone did.

Cole wasn't here yet.

For the first hour everyone had kept a close eye on

the gate, so certain that he would attend. Who could resist this crowd? Now, they weren't so sure.

They started the grills and brought out the food. The party continued and laughter and heated discussions abounded. Parents were helping kids with their plates in the food line when Will yelled, "He's here!"

A collective breath was drawn at the first glimpse of the dark-haired man rounding the corner of the house. Seeing that it was Marsh Sullivan, everyone's collective breath became a collective sigh, which prompted Marsh to say, "Sorry we're late. Julia was resting."

Carrying their son, he kept a protective hand on his new wife's back. Julia Sullivan wore a peach-colored ball cap that didn't fully conceal her baldness. Although there were dark smudges beneath her eyes, she smiled regally all around and said, "I'll try not to let it happen again."

Guests swarmed the couple. Gabby Avery gave one-and-a-half-year-old Joey a cookie and April brought Marsh and Julia a beverage. JoAnn Avery, the matriarch of them all, led the couple to the shaded patio. After shooing her oldest grandson out of one of the chairs, she fussed until she was satisfied that Julia was comfortable.

"How are you feeling?" she asked.

"Other than tiring easily, I'm feeling great," Julia replied.

"Of course she's feeling great," Julia's sister-in-law Lacey insisted. "The big *C* is gone."

"Kaput," a neighbor said.

"Good riddance," Marsh added, worry creeping across his face.

"Not just gone," Lacey exclaimed. "That sniveling

breast cancer has been annihilated. It wouldn't dare come back."

For all the agreeable responses, everyone knew it was too soon to rest easy, even though everyone pretended for Marsh and Julia's sake.

Burgers were loaded onto buns and plates heaped high. All the while, a dozen pairs of eyes kept watch for one more guest to walk through the gate.

Another hour passed. As the sun eased toward the western horizon, the party began showing signs of winding down. Ice cream treats were doled out to everyone, and as was the custom near the end of every Avery outdoor gathering, Will and Ben brought out a plastic tub filled with water balloons. After listening to a quick recitation of rules set by their parents, Gracie and Violet and each of their cousins and neighbors grabbed a handful of water balloons. And the screeching resumed.

April sank into a chair at the patio table. And sighed. She told herself she shouldn't be disappointed Cole hadn't joined them. He'd never said he would come.

But she'd thought—

She'd hoped—

For what, a miracle? Apparently it would have taken a miracle to bring him here to meet this kindhearted crowd.

"Cole's not coming," her best friend, Lacey said, pushing her dark hair out of her face and breaking into April's reverie.

Casting a wistful glance at the open gate, April shook her head. "It doesn't look like it."

"I'm surprised he didn't join us," her mother-in-law declared. She pointed at her two surviving sons who were sneaking behind Noah's back. "But the antics of those two don't surprise me in the least."

Alerted as if by some sixth sense, Lacey's husband glanced behind him then zigzagged like a jackrabbit. The two water balloons that would have soaked the back of his shirt burst in the grass six feet away. Every woman at the table saw Noah gage the distance between him and the tub of water balloons, and knew he was planning his retaliation.

"The difference between men and boys," Lacey said.

"Does anybody see any difference?" Gabby Avery smiled as Ben and his brother continued their dogged pursuit of Noah.

One of the balloons found its mark on the back of Noah's head. Cold water running down his neck, he let out a yell that drew even the kids' attention.

Noah snagged the next balloon out of thin air without popping it and hurled it back. The front of his T-shirt now wet, too, Ben yelled to his brother. "Get him, Will!"

"So tell us, April," her mother-in-law said. "What's Cole Cavanaugh like?"

April knew what she was really asking, for it had to do with the bond Cole and Jay had shared. JoAnn Avery had always been pretty and petite. Inside she was strong as nails. The past year had left a lingering fragility in her eyes and across her shoulders. All six of the Avery offspring had inherited their hazel eyes and stature from their father, but it was a well-known fact that their affinity for pranks came directly from their mother's branch on the family tree.

"Cole's tall and quiet and very intense," April said. "He's kind to Gracie and Violet, but I have yet to see him smile, really smile."

A movement near the house drew her attention. Her breath caught, for it seemed another guest was joining the party after all, this one dark-haired and raw-boned and intense.

"Don't take my word for it," she said, wonder softening her voice. "He just walked through the gate."

While the women turned to look, Will and Ben pitched water balloons at Noah, who was still pledging retaliation. Keeping his eyes on his pursuers, he didn't see the man behind him, and ducked four feet in front of the unsuspecting newcomer.

A gasp went through the crowd, because Cole Cavanaugh was about to get soaked.

Chapter Five

Cars still lined April's street when Cole arrived at her place Sunday evening. Hurrying, he followed the sounds of hardy yells and laughter around the side of the house. He'd prepared to be bombarded by Jay's family the minute he entered the backyard.

He wasn't expecting the water balloons that were coming right at him.

He hit his knees. The first two balloons sailed over his head. The third nicked his elbow, wetting his sleeve and sending a cool mist into the air.

Cole had an eye for detail and quickly cataloged the group of guests gathered in the backyard the same way he'd gauged the speed and direction of those balloons. There were a dozen kids running around and nearly twenty adults present. April was the only one in yellow. She seemed to have frozen along with the others.

Before his injury, rising from his knees and springing to his feet would have been a painless, effortless proposition. He could still get up. It was just a matter of remembering to lead with his right foot as if rising from a genuflection. He was in the process of starting the maneuver when a man with graying hair came forward and extended his hand. As Cole squinted into the sun, something deep inside him went perfectly still, for he suddenly knew how Jay would have looked in thirty-five years.

This wasn't the way he'd planned to meet Jay's father, but he took the hand without hesitation. On his feet again, he said, "Thank you, sir."

Jim Avery had a full head of gray hair. He'd passed his build and hazel eyes on to his son. In his late sixties now, Jay's father was one of those men who would stand proud and handsome into his eighties; he also had a strong grip and a steady gaze.

Cole had rehearsed what he would say to this man, but before he could even begin, Mr. Avery cuffed him on the arm and called, "Somebody get this boy a plate of food." With that, he stepped aside to give the rest of the guests their turn.

Cole found April with his gaze. She gave him a tentative smile, but didn't come forward to make introductions. It was better this way. He was here, alone. It was best that everyone saw that.

The next person to shake his hand had dark shaggy hair, a genuine smile and a swagger that had former troublemaker written all over it. "Noah Sullivan," he said. "That was close. You have good reflexes."

"It takes one to know one," Cole replied.

Jay's brother Ben shouldered Noah aside and introduced himself and his wife, Gabby, a savvy strawberry blonde with brown eyes and a ready smile. Somebody brought around a cooler filled with beverages and someone else handed him a plate of food even though he'd insisted he'd already eaten. He took a bite of a burger to be polite then put the plate down.

A tall, intense man named Marsh Sullivan introduced Cole to a fragile-looking woman wearing a pink ball cap, and a sturdy baby named Joey. Cole didn't know what color Julia Sullivan's hair would be when it grew back, but her eyes were blue, her bearing proud. She may have been pale, but she had a fighter's smile. It humbled him, and reminded him that there was more than one kind of war.

Cole's hand was shaken, his cheek kissed. Always, he was aware of April's whereabouts.

While he met two of Jay's sisters and their husbands, April was holding an unbelievably tiny baby. As he showed Jay's brothers the drawing of the plans for April's remodel, she picked up plates. He was flanked by two of her neighbors who were telling him about new car dealership south of town and the best place to get a cup of coffee in Orchard Hill when she bent down to tie Violet's shoe. He noticed the way her dress fit and the way the sun reflected off something shiny in her hair.

More than anything, he noticed that she met his gaze from wherever she was, and each time it happened, he felt a greater pull. He wanted her. But after his heart-to-heart talk at Jay's grave yesterday, he was more determined than ever to keep it to himself.

Turning his attention to April's guests, he spoke with Lacey Sullivan, who was expecting twins anytime, and did his best to pay close attention when Gracie and Violet introduced the other children at the party. There was a boy named Zachary, two girls, Maddie and JoJo, Maddie's puppy, Rascal, and a passel of other kids who were more interested in playing than introductions.

After meeting nearly everyone, he found a quiet spot near the food table where April stood surveying her backyard. The tops of her shoulders were pink, her hair lifting in the soft breeze. Man, she was pretty.

"Are you taking a breather, too?" she asked.

"Something like that." He accepted the can of ginger ale she held out to him, and felt the thrum run up his arm when his fingers brushed hers. When it didn't stop at his arm, he reeled his awareness in. He could do this. He'd fought, he'd bled, he'd lost. He'd survived. Surely resisting this attraction to Jay's widow would be one more thing he survived. He'd made a promise to Jay on that battlefield, and doing so had brought him a small portion of peace. That was why he'd come to Orchard Hill, to April.

He wanted her, though. More than he'd ever dreamed he would.

April sensed a dozen pairs of eyes on her as she finally came face-to-face with Cole. She'd intended to be the first to greet him when he arrived, but when Jay's father gave Cole a hand getting up, she'd hung back, giving them their moment. After that, he handled introductions on his own. He may have preferred small groups, but no matter what he said, he was good with people.

He was a hero, and she staked no proprietary claim on him. He wasn't hers. Of course he wasn't hers. But whether he knew it yet or not, the moment he'd placed his hand in her father-in-law's, he'd become one of them.

She hadn't recovered from witnessing the silent exchange. Her breathing felt shallower and her heart beat stronger. It was as if she'd turned a corner in the dark, lonely tunnel she'd been lost in, and could suddenly see a light up ahead.

Her guests had children to put to bed and work in the morning, yet they'd stayed to meet Cole. Some had spoken to him alone, others in pairs. All came away swallowing hard or blinking back tears.

Cole had to know how much his presence meant to everyone. She couldn't be certain what meeting them meant to him, for he kept his expression carefully schooled. He was attentive to whomever he was listening to, but guarded.

What was he guarding?

He tipped his can of ginger ale up, and she saw that his knuckles were scraped. There was nothing unusual about that, or about his faded jeans and blue cotton shirt, the sleeves rolled halfway up his forearms. It wasn't his appearance that changed the rhythm of her heartbeat. This went far deeper than that.

"You must have found my note," she said, because she couldn't go on staring at him forever no matter how much he intrigued her.

"And Gracie's and Violet's artwork. I have two complete sets of my own now."

She liked the deep timbre of his voice, liked the shape of his mouth and the dark coffee color of his hair. She especially liked the way his eyes darkened every time they delved into hers.

"I swear your door wasn't locked yesterday. It opened

by itself on a cross breeze. I called your name. I really did try to wake you," she said.

"I thought I was dreaming."

"I didn't think you were going to make it to the party."

"I intended to get here earlier, but I helped Kyle Merrick cut up the tree uprooted in the storm, and time got away from us. I didn't mean to keep your guests waiting."

Her *guests*, and not *her*? she wondered. He'd made the distinction and she'd noticed.

"You were right about this crowd," he said. "So far I've received a quick education on the weather, the fluctuating market value of apples, the art of flying, swollen ankles, the last race for town council and at least ten potential problems with my plan for your upstairs."

"I told you. And did they share some memory of Jay?"

He nodded. "Obviously there are sides to him I didn't know."

She got lost for a moment in the depth in his eyes.

"There's still one person I haven't met."

"Yes." April wasn't surprised he'd been keeping track. "Jay's mom wants you to know she's been saving the best for last for you."

April thought about warning Cole that her mother-in-law was a force to be reckoned with. She was helpful, forward, kind and often said exactly what she was thinking. But Cole was a grown man, strong and capable of handling himself.

They walked to the patio together, their shadows gliding across the grass ahead of them. Their shoulders didn't brush, their elbows didn't touch, and yet she felt a connection. She didn't know what she was going to do about it, and panicked a little when she thought about doing anything, but it was there, a soft thrum, a steady lure out of the darkness.

Several guests had started gathering up their children and dishes and coolers. Every one of them stopped to watch Cole meet Jay's mother. It was a wonder they couldn't see April's heart beating as she stopped next to the table where JoAnn Avery was sitting.

"Mother," April said. "This is—"

"I've got it, honey." With that, her mother-in-law rose fluidly to her feet and faced Cole. "You've probably noticed we don't stand on ceremony around here. I'm JoAnn. It's nice to meet my son's dearest friend."

Everyone expected her to kiss his cheek, but nobody expected to hear her whisper, "My granddaughters tell me you sleep in the buff. A man after my own heart." Jay's mother had a whisper that could penetrate steel.

April's mouth dropped open. "What she meant was—"

But her mother-in-law interrupted. "For heaven's sakes, there's nothing wrong with sleeping in the nude. It's my sleeping attire of choice."

Jay's sisters gasped as if that was more information than they needed about their parents; a couple of the guys chuckled and Lacey laughed out loud. Cole's only concession to surprise in JoAnn Avery's extremely personal topic was the slight lift of one eyebrow and a slow, beguiling grin. "I wasn't expecting company, ma'am."

April peered at Gracie and Violet, who stood on either side of their grandmother like twin angels. "Girls, did you tell anyone else?"

Their eyes were large, but they stood mute, the equivalent of them taking the fifth.

"They might have mentioned it to me," Lacey admitted.

"And me," Jay's father said.

"And us," two of April's sisters-in-law said.

April floundered. "I'm sure nobody means… That is, the girls and I didn't intend to invade your privacy, Cole…"

Jay's mother patted Cole's cheek. "You don't feel invaded, do you?" With a wink, she said, "Isn't this better than me blubbering all over you? Just between you and me, the only thing better than sleeping nude is swimming that way."

And that started a round of gasps and exclamations from JoAnn's daughters. JoAnn waved them away as if she were swatting at a bothersome mosquito.

"At least three of your neighbors can see your pool from their houses. They would be able to see you swimming without any clothes on, Mom," Jay's sister Elizabeth pointed out.

"No one your dad and I know has night vision, honey."

"You *and* Dad?" one sister said.

"Then at least this was at night?" the other one added.

"Sometimes, dear."

As blonde and pretty as her sister, Regan clamped her mouth shut as any horrified daughter would. "I'm not going to tell Ryan about this," she said. "His dream is to swim at nude beaches."

"Tell me what?"

"That it's time to go," Regan replied as her husband

snaked his arm around her shoulder. "Where are the kids?"

"We should be going, too," Jay's mother said, turning to April. Several other guests got up. "I'm afraid I'm clearing the room, dear."

The lines that had formed beside JoAnn Avery's eyes and mouth this past year irked her to no end. She wore her sadness, bore it, but she wouldn't allow it to own her. April admired her more than she could say.

Giving her a hug, she said, "You're something else, do you know that? Love you."

"I know you do." JoAnn smiled serenely at April and touched Cole's arm. "I'm glad you could join us tonight, young man. Jay was friendly to most everyone, but only a select few were his chosen friends. Now I've gone and gotten something in my eye."

Everyone who heard her suddenly had something in his or her eye, too.

JoAnn glanced around the yard. "It looks like Jim's ready. Will and Kristy are packing up the kids and the coolers, too. Good night, everybody."

The yard cleared out quickly after that, for most of the adults had to work in the morning. A lost shoe was found, children were gathered, hugs given, trash thrown away, a Frisbee rescued from the garage roof, chairs folded up and hauled out by whoever had brought them.

And then, suddenly, Cole was the only one left. It was nearly nine-thirty and Gracie and Violet were crouched together, their heads touching as they studied a cicada crawling in the grass. It would be dark soon, but April was in no hurry to lure them from their discovery.

Cole stood watching them. And April watched him.

His shoulders were back, his weight on his right leg, his eyes on the girls. The lingering sunlight cast him in silhouette, cottonwood fluff from a neighbor's tree drifting weightlessly on the air all around him.

He was undeniably handsome, his nose straight, his chin strong and his chest broad. Cole was all sharp angles and hard planes, his back straight, his shirt tucked neatly in.

He turned as if he'd felt her looking at him, and started toward her without so much as a hint of a smile on his face.

"You made a liar out of me tonight," she said.

He did a double take, and she hurried to explain.

"Before you arrived, Jay's mom asked me what you're like, and I told her you're determined and decent but don't smile readily, and yet you laughed out loud with her. Who knew she and Jay's dad go skinny-dipping?"

"She told me that to put me at ease," he said.

April wondered what her mother-in-law's secret was, because Cole definitely was not at ease now. If she didn't do something in the next few seconds, he was going to flee. And she didn't want him to leave yet.

"Would you come in for a few minutes?" Sensing his hesitation, she added, "I'm curious about those changes you said Jay's brothers made to your blueprint."

Her ploy worked. As she led the way into the house, she thought her beguiling mother-in-law wasn't the only one with a few tricks up her sleeve.

Cole wasn't sure how it had happened. He'd been about to take his leave, and now he was explaining the Averys' somewhat confusing suggestions for her floor plan. They held the sheet of paper together, their heads almost as close as Gracie's and Violet's were as they studied the bug.

She listened closely as he pointed out each of the penciled lines drawn by various members of her extended family. There was a larger closet here, another doorway there, an entirely different location for the enormous bathroom. Evidently, his explanation was making sense. How was a mystery, because all he could think about was how feminine April looked in yellow, how soft her hair felt where it brushed his arm, and how much he wished—

No, he wouldn't allow the thought to fully form.

She'd secured her hair away from her face on one side. The style bared her ear, the length of her neck and the delicate edge of her collarbone. He lost his train of thought as he imagined pressing his lips to each of those places. Again, he consciously reeled his wayward thoughts to safer territory.

Thankfully, she went to the door and called, "Girls, it's getting dark out. It's time to come inside. Leave the bug alone now. He's tired and wants to go to bed."

The twins jumped up from their squatting positions and raced to the house. "It's already dead," Gracie said.

"Because you squished it," Violet grumbled, letting the door slam behind her and her sister. In the kitchen now, she wrinkled her nose up at Cole. "She always squishes bugs. Gross."

Though Cole's laugh sounded rusty, it released some of the pent-up tension that had become lodged below his ribs. April was right. He wasn't prone to smiles; he laughed even less.

She sent the girls to wash their hands and put on

their pajamas, and asked him if he would like anything. "Decaf, pop, a beer, water, leftovers?"

He eyed the pan of brownies longingly, but said, "I don't need anything, thanks."

She put two brownies on a small plate anyway, added a clean fork and handed it all to him. "There's milk in the fridge. Help yourself to anything else." With that, she left the room.

He heard a drawer closing and water running; she was helping Violet and Gracie get ready for bed. Eyeing the plate on the table, he forked a bite into his mouth. The brownies were gooey and laced with chunks of fudge and swirls of cream cheese. He finished both, and since he didn't see a dishwasher, he piled the plate on top of the other dishes stacked in the sink.

In the bathroom, April was instructing the girls to brush their teeth. Cole shook his head because they did more talking than brushing. Leaving the floor plan on the table, he tied the trash bag and carried it out to the garage. Back inside, he wandered to a bookcase in the living room and picked up a framed photo of April dressed in white, Jay in a dark suit and tie.

He stared until their faces blurred and the ache in his chest grew so heavy he couldn't breathe. Next, he looked at pictures of Gracie and Violet at various ages. There was also an old photo of an attractive couple and two young girls who had to be April and her sister, and other framed photos of people he'd met today.

He could hear prayers being said in a room down the hall. There was of a lot of *God blessing*, and other bits of conversation he couldn't quite hear. And then April came to the doorway. "They'd like you to tell them good night in private."

He'd never tucked a child in, and wasn't sure where to begin. Beneath the glow of a star-shaped night-light, he was careful not to step on the toys on the floor, and went to Gracie's bed first. She looked up and gave him a sleepy smile.

"Good night," he said for lack of a better idea.

Evidently it was enough. Her eyes already drifting closed, she tucked a tattered stuffed rabbit under her chin and murmured, "'Night, Cole."

He moved to the edge of Violet's bed next. He'd barely sat down before she said, "Mama says if I take off my pajamas I can't wear my princess dress for a week. I wish I had a puppy like Maddie's. Mama says maybe, but that always means no. Would you ask her? I'd take care of her all by myself. I'd name her Jasmine. Or Belle, or Arielle, or maybe Beu—"

Her voice trailed away and the list of potential names went unfinished. That quickly, she'd fallen asleep, too.

He found April in the kitchen washing dishes, and watched her from the doorway for a moment. She'd brushed her hair, an odd thing to notice, but he saw details like that. Every inch of her countertops was covered with leftovers and empty serving dishes and silverware and pitchers and more. He wondered if he should offer to help. What was the protocol here?

"You know," he said, entering the room. "Violet looks like you, but I'll bet Jay's mother was a lot like her as a child."

He'd expected April to laugh or smile or at least nod, but she simply continued washing dishes.

"Just a heads-up, she isn't giving up on her wish for a puppy." He came to stand near the dish drainer on the counter. "She's already choosing a name."

April sighed.

"You don't like dogs?"

"Oh, I love dogs. My sister and I had one when we were kids. Marilee named her Lady Godiva, but our parents made her shorten it to Lady." She sighed again.

"Long day?" he asked.

She shrugged one shoulder. "How were the fudge brownies?"

"Good. Really good."

"Lacey made them. They're called Better Than Sex Brownies. That's the honest to God truth. She showed me the recipe on her phone."

"I said they were good," he said. "But I wouldn't go that far."

Again, he was surprised April didn't even crack a smile. It was dark outside, and he could see her reflection in the window over the sink. He considered bringing up Jay. Was she missing him? Was that it? Did being with his family make her miss him more? Or was spending time with Cole responsible for that?

"Is everything okay?" he asked.

Her nod wasn't convincing.

He eased closer and touched her shoulder, his gaze following the delicate stitching around the neckline of her dress. How many times must he force his eyes elsewhere?

"What's wrong, April?"

"What makes you ask?"

"You've washed that glass three times."

She finally looked up at him, but she didn't give him so much as a hint about what was bothering her. Instead, from out of the blue she kissed him.

Her lips touched his lightly, little more than a brush

of air, so soft that the sweetness of it made it impossible for him to pull away. His eyes slammed shut and his breath caught.

She must have gone up on her tiptoes, for he was tall and she wasn't. Her body rested lightly against his, fitting him perfectly. She was lithe, warm and so incredibly brave. He was drowning in her scent, in her kiss, in her beauty and in her.

Her touch was a connection, a meeting of lips, a melding of desires and sensations. Warmth swirled all around him, circling like an echo, more vibration than sound, more magic than he'd known in a long time.

She tilted her face slightly; her hands fluttered to his shoulders, her body soft as only a woman could be. Desire churned inside him as his hands found their way around her back, his fingers threading through the loose, silken curls in her hair. From far in the distance a clock struck ten. The wind sighed and night insects chirruped, but April made no sound. There was no groan deep in her throat, no whimper, no request, certainly no demand for anything other than this breathy connection.

On and on it went, his heart hammering in his chest, his lips opening over hers. His senses spun in ten directions at once, but each and every one of them circled back to where his mouth covered hers.

He loved touching her hair, relished the smooth soft texture of her skin. Her curves were lush, her thighs braced between his. He hadn't expected this, hadn't been prepared for it. He'd dreamed of it, though, of kissing her and holding her and learning her by heart. His dreams hadn't done this justice.

That thought took root inside his skull, unfurling

until it broke through the clouds in his mind. He'd dreamed of this a long time ago, and he'd always felt guilty as sin about it.

The realization had him dragging his mouth from hers.

Her eyes fluttered open, pools of gold. Her cheeks were pink, her lips wet and parted, as if in wonder. If he laid his fingertip over the vein pulsing at the base of her neck, he knew her heartbeat would match his.

Desire and honor warred within him. He wanted to kiss her again, to breathe her in, to draw her up and lay her down. He wanted to press himself over her and lose himself in her.

"April."

"I know. I shouldn't have done that."

He shouldn't have done that. He'd told himself just this afternoon he wouldn't. He'd promised. And not just himself.

He should have stopped her before it began. He sure as hell shouldn't have encouraged her, but he knew there was nothing he could have done to keep from responding.

He reeled himself back a step, then two. Now that he was too far away to touch her, maybe he would be able to think.

She was lonely. That was all this was. Acute loneliness. He understood loneliness. But he couldn't lead her on in any way.

"You could be married for all I know," she said. "Jay said you weren't, but that was fourteen months ago. If you are, I'm so sorry. I wouldn't have kissed you if I'd known. I should have asked before I did."

"I'm not married, April."

"Fourteen months," she said as if he hadn't spoken. "Jay's only been gone fourteen months. I told myself maybe in fourteen years. But not now."

"You're right. Not now," he said, his voice gravelly. He could still see the effects of their shared passion in her eyes, on her lips, and the buds of her breasts her clothing couldn't conceal.

"That was what I told myself all evening," she said. "It's too soon. But then you dove to your knees out of sheer instinct and dodged those water balloons, and you placed your hand in Jay's father's. Do you have any idea what a gift you gave him by doing that? And you let Jay's brothers shake your hand and his sisters kiss your cheek, and you smiled for Jay's mom. Each time, something inside me shifted. And I wanted to feel my hand in yours. I wanted to look into your eyes up close. I wanted to see you smile at me and I wanted to experience your kiss."

"April, I shouldn't have—I never intended—"

"I'm not asking you to kiss me again, Cole."

He released the breath he'd been holding. Okay then, this was just something she'd needed to experience once. Now they could move on. His promise was safe after all—

"But I wish you would."

He must have heard wrong. It was a miracle he could hear anything over the roaring in his ears. But he hadn't been mistaken. She wanted another kiss. It was in the gold-flecked brown eyes looking at him, in her chin as she raised it, in the soft smile on her lips.

He was across the kitchen in three strides, but instead of wrapping his arms around her and hauling her against him like in some overwritten movie script, he placed a hand on either side of her face and brought his mouth to hers.

Her breath caught; his deepened. He swayed closer; she sighed. He held her face in his hands, her hair silky beneath his fingers; her mouth opened beneath his. Kissing her changed the very air he breathed and the rhythm of his heart. He wanted this, wanted her, more than he'd ever wanted anything in his life.

He'd tried to tell himself he'd been too long without a woman, but the truth was he could have taken a fellow guest at the inn up on her offer just last night. He hadn't, though. There was only one woman he wanted.

He fought his natural instinct to ease April backward until the wall was at her back, to touch her bare skin. Instead, he held his position in the middle of her kitchen, his feet straddling hers.

This kiss was enough. It was everything.

She flicked her tongue over his lower lip, and it set off an explosion and brought a groan from a place deep inside him. Her mouth was wet, her curves woman-soft, her scent intoxicating.

"I wish I didn't have to breathe," she whispered, but she took a ragged breath, her head tipping back.

"I know," he rasped against her throat.

She made a sound, half hum, half groan, and he felt the vibration beneath his lips. She laughed; apparently he'd discovered a ticklish spot. He found her mouth again, and for just a moment he felt her smile against his lips, but it dissolved as the kiss deepened. Her hands came to rest on his upper arms, her body resting more fully against him. His blood thickened and his need deepened.

It was a kiss of discovery, a kiss of two lonely people

finding solace in something beautiful and honest and irresistible. It slowed gradually, lips yielding, seeking, only to yield once again. After they broke the kiss, he raised his head and she lowered hers. He eased backward and she rocked back down from her toes.

He watched as she smoothed her dress and hair. In a voice far raspier than it had been five minutes ago, he said, "You surprised me with the first kiss. I take full responsibility for the second one. I don't know what to say except I'm sorry."

April stopped straightening her dress and looked at him.

She was the one who'd asked for that kiss. Why was he apologizing for it?

"I didn't come here for this," he said. "Not to Orchard Hill. Certainly not to 404 Baldwin Street."

She had a dozen questions, but she focused on the most important one. "Why did you come here?" she asked.

He stood mute to the count of five then said, "I came to put something right with Jay."

Her heart was still fluttering wildly, and she didn't know what to do with her hands as she waited for Cole to explain. She settled for clasping them in front of her.

Getting information out of him was like pulling weeds. Some came out readily but most broke off just below the surface. He wasn't like other men she knew. Goodness, half the people in her life shared far more information than she wanted or needed.

Cole was different. He was guarded. But he wasn't immune to her.

"Don't get me wrong," he said. "The fact that you wanted me to kiss you was the finest compliment I've had in years. I know how important Jay was to you. If you're ready to start looking for a new future, fourteen months isn't too soon, not at all. Good for you. I mean that. You're too fine a woman, and too damn pretty to be alone forever."

April opened her mouth to speak, but Cole gave her no opportunity to interrupt.

"I don't want to hurt your feelings," he said. "But I won't step into Jay's shoes, or take his place even temporarily. I'll understand if you'd rather find someone else to renovate your upstairs."

April fought down a sudden rising panic. Without letting it show, she said, "I would have thought, as Jay's best friend, you were a man of your word."

He did a double take. Just as quickly, his shoulders went back, his chin rose and his jaw set stubbornly. "I am, and I think you know it."

He wasn't an easy man to intimidate. He wasn't an easy man, period, but at least neither of them was backing out of the renovation project. She didn't understand on an intellectual level, but instinctively she knew that building something lasting was important, perhaps imperative to both their futures.

She saw him to the door. "Our agreement stands," she said. "You should know I've decided I want two bedrooms upstairs instead of one, with a connecting bathroom between them. While the guys were suggesting improvements to make the master suite more luxuriant, we girls were discussing whether it's wise for me to sleep upstairs and the girls downstairs when they're teenagers. I'll need to think about curfews then and a host of other teenage issues, and I think it would be best if I sleep downstairs and they're upstairs. We can talk more in the morning."

He stared at her long enough to make the average person squirm. She held her ground and his gaze unfailingly.

"All right, April. We'll talk in the morning."

Somehow she didn't believe he was referring to her new floor plan. She closed the door but left the outside light on until she saw him pull away from the curb out front. Covering her eyes with the palms of her hands, she took a deep breath. It did nothing to calm her galloping heart.

She made sure the doors were locked then eyed the littered counters and the sink filled with dishes. Leaving them for now, she wandered through her quiet house. She checked on the girls and saw that each was covered with a sheet. Cole must have done that when he told them good-night.

Before she'd kissed him.

She'd kissed him. She hardly recognized the woman who did that.

She reminded herself that it was just a kiss. Technically it had been more than one kiss, but she wasn't going to argue with herself over minor details.

There were far more important matters to deal with. She'd been imagining Cole's kiss since the moment he'd arrived tonight but she'd never intended to actually instigate it. Their second kiss had been even more beautiful, and yet when it ended, something went unfinished.

Cole hadn't come here to step into Jay's shoes. Was that what he truly believed would happen if they had an affair? Her hands flew to her cheeks at the thought.

No one said anything about an affair.

But Cole was here. And there was a reason for that.

And she wished she could relive that second kiss. She remembered when he'd told her he didn't dream anymore, and yet he'd thought he'd been dreaming yesterday when she'd gone to his room at the inn to leave him a note. She hadn't dreamed in a very long time, either. She almost wished she would just so she could dream about that kiss.

She'd always had a quirky side but she'd never been the aggressive type. The guys she'd dated before she met Jay had pursued her. With Jay, the attraction had been mutual and immediate. When she buried him, she thought she would never kiss another man as long as she lived.

She only had to close her eyes to see her young husband's handsome face, his hazel eyes crinkled at the corners, a smile on his lips, so much joy just waiting to be let out. Her chest felt hollow as she turned on the lamp on the table beside her bed.

From there she padded to her bedroom door and touched Jay's robe. Bringing the soft fabric to her face, she sighed, for his scent was all but gone now. She tried to recreate it in her mind. He was the first dandelion in new grass, that courageous faint ray of sunshine that melted the last tuft of snow. She could describe it perfectly, and yet try as she might, she couldn't conjure up his actual scent. The knowledge brought a lump to her throat and a physical pang to her heart.

She slipped his robe on over her dress. Pushing the sleeves up, she drew the lapels together and padded out of her bedroom. Tracing her lips with the tips of three fingers, she looked in on the girls again and quietly drew their door closed.

If Jay hadn't died, she never would have kissed another man. She truly believed she never would have wanted to. Hugging his bathrobe to her, she ached with love and useless longing.

If only she could will him back, but she could no more bring him back than she could recreate his scent. Her heart thudded, and a tear trailed down her cheek.

She wandered aimlessly through her house, and finally ended up at the top of the stairs. Turning on the light, she tried to imagine this space the way it would look after Cole finished, but she couldn't see past the bare rafters and dusty plywood floors.

She turned the lights off and retraced her footsteps to her bedroom where she slipped Jay's robe off and lovingly hung it on the hook where it had been since he'd left, never to return. She drew in a shuddering breath, and caught a whiff of a brisk clean scent she associated with winter.

She would always miss Jay, would always love him, but it was Cole's scent that was on her clothes, Cole's kiss that was on her lips, the memory of it that was in her bloodstream and on her mind.

She knew what it meant when a man set his jaw the way Cole had tonight. He had no intention of repeating what had happened between them no matter how much he'd enjoyed it, needed it or wanted it.

She'd enjoyed it, too, far more in fact than she ever would have believed possible. She'd felt a stirring of desire she'd thought would never resurface; she'd seen a light behind her closed eyes she'd thought had been extinguished forever.

April didn't know what she was going to do about

it, for he'd made his intentions clear. He wouldn't be kissing her again. He'd been pretty adamant about that.

She sighed, for if she were given the chance, she was pretty sure she would try to change his mind about that. Already, she wanted another kiss. Somewhere deep inside her a tiny seed had been planted.

She could already feel it taking root. From it grew a yearning for something deeper than mere kisses.

Chapter Six

*I*t was one of those mild summer afternoons that couldn't help but put a smile on April's face. The air in downtown Orchard Hill was balmy, the breeze was gentle and the freshly mown grass on the town square was fragrant and lush.

She strolled hand-in-hand with Gracie and Violet listening to their happy chatter. Feeling as carefree as the cotton candy clouds in the sky, she didn't find it startling that she could see her daughters' eyes through their princess sunglasses, for nothing felt odd today, not the balmy weather, not the exotic flowers in hues she'd never seen blooming amid the usual daisies, petunias and trailing sweet potato vines growing in planters beside every door.

It didn't feel strange to see clouds edged in lavender, pink and yellow or that cars glided soundlessly down *the street as if on currents of air. Even the melodic voices of a children's choir on a distant hill seemed fitting somehow, as did her fleeting glimpse of her father rehearsing for his next sermon on glistening marble stairs. She drank in the sight of him, for she hadn't seen him in ten years.*

People she didn't recognize were gathered around him, and others formed a circle around the bronze sculpture of Johnny Appleseed someone had mysteriously donated to Orchard Hill some seventy years ago. Near the fountain two women with white hair and silver dresses were reading aloud in lilting voices.

From somewhere far away came a jarring pounding that threatened to draw her from this peaceful moment. She ignored the racket and continued to stroll along the winding sidewalk where she was surrounded by her happy daughters and melodious music and tranquil light.

She didn't question why Cole was with them or why he was wearing his army fatigues, of all things. He smiled at her, and her heart felt as light and full as the helium-filled clouds overhead.

The knocking sounded again, louder and even more jarring. It drew attention to the subtle oddities all around her. Why were the clouds colored in soft hues and why was her father here and who were those people at the fountain and where was all the normal daily noise?

All at once the clouds darkened and the exotic flowers shriveled up all around her. Car engines roared like thunder, lights flashed and her father disappeared, as did the children's choir. Cole broke away and darted into the street and called a name she couldn't hear for the screeching of brakes and shattering of glass.

"Noooo!"

There came an ominous thud, and always, far away, pounding, pounding, pounding.

April bolted upright in bed.

Her heart raced so fast it seemed to rise up, strangling the scream in her throat. She looked around, trying to get her bearings. It wasn't afternoon and she wasn't on the town square and there were no vibrantly colored flowers or cotton candy clouds. It was morning and she was in her bedroom. Jay's robe was on the hook behind the door and a novel was open on her nightstand and her sheets were tangled around her legs.

She'd been dreaming.

Her heart still racing, she realized it was the first time she'd dreamed since Jay died. She rubbed her eyes, pushed her hair out of her face and tried to extricate her legs from the sheet.

All these months, she'd thought that if she ever dreamed again it would contain some sweet memory of Jay. Or perhaps her dreams would be silly, like the time she dreamed she was a parakeet, and that time she dreamed her goldfish could talk. Sometimes her dreams were otherworldly like that time she dreamed she could fly. Before her father died she'd dreamed of a huge funeral and once, before she even knew she was pregnant, she'd dreamed she would have twins. She'd had other dreams that seemed to foretell the future, but those two stood out.

She froze at the ominous implication. The screeching brakes, the honking horns, the shattering glass, the horrendous discordant crunch of a car buckling on impact. And Cole, suddenly gone.

It had been a dream, nothing more.

She said it to herself. And then she said it out loud. "It was just a dream, only a dream." It might have meant something but it hadn't been prophetic. And that was final.

The pounding came again. That sound was real. Someone was knocking on her back door.

She squinted at the clock on her bedside table. Lunging closer, she looked again.

It couldn't be. But the clock didn't lie. It was after eight. Cole was due to arrive any minute. It was probably him knocking on her door. At last she had something resembling a rational thought.

She freed her feet from the final snag in the sheet and stumbled out of bed. Starting one way and then the other, she got hold of herself and darted out to the kitchen where she could see the silhouette of a man behind the blinds on the door.

"Just one minute," she called loudly.

Dashing back down the hall, she looked in on the girls, who were normally up with the sun. This morning they were still fast asleep. Evidently yesterday's party had worn them out. She raced to her room where she stripped off her short nightgown and dressed faster than she had in years. In the bathroom, she splashed water on her face, brushed her teeth and ran a comb through her hair.

She was still flustered when she peeked behind the blinds, but at least she was presentable enough to open the door for Cole.

He took one look at her, and whatever else he'd been about to say was replaced with, "What's wrong?"

She shook her head.

"What happened?"

She still couldn't speak.

"Is it the girls?"

"No," she finally managed to say. "They're still asleep."

As she backed up a step, and then another, she saw the quick once-over he gave her before cautiously coming inside. She'd dressed without looking in the mirror, and glanced down to make sure everything was zipped and buttoned and covered. The shorts had been the first pair she came to in her drawer. They were white and a little shorter than those she normally wore but not risqué. Her fitted jade top was buttoned correctly, and although she hadn't taken the time to slip into shoes, everything else was in its rightful place.

Except her heart. That was still lodged in her throat.

Cole carried his laptop beneath one arm. Looking around her kitchen, which was immaculate this morning, he said, "Did you get any sleep at all?"

"A little."

"How little?" he asked.

"I slept long enough to dream," she said. Reminding herself to breathe, she said, "It's the first time I dreamed since Jay died."

She read surprise on his face at her admission, and remembered when he'd told her he hadn't dreamed since Jay died, either. "Was it a nightmare?" he asked.

"It didn't start out that way, but it turned into one."

Why couldn't she have relived Cole's kiss in her dreams? Who was that woman who had been so certain of herself just hours ago? How could she have kissed Cole last night? How could she have opened herself up to such intense feelings? The possibility of such painful loss?

She backed away; she might have wound up in the living room if the counter hadn't stopped her backward retreat. "You're right," she said, her eyes darting to his. "Last night was a mistake."

"It's okay, April."

"It's not okay. I thought last night was a new beginning. I was wrong. It's not your—I shouldn't have—"

She knew she was rambling but she couldn't help it. Maybe she *was* freaking out, but she was scared.

Logically, she knew she was overreacting. For heaven's sake, she'd once dreamed she was a parakeet. That hadn't exactly come true, now, had it? That didn't change her reaction to her dream last night. She felt the aftereffects even now. She hadn't recovered from losing Jay. She couldn't bear to experience that kind of loss again.

Without saying another word, Cole turned on his heel and walked out the door he'd just entered. Standing there in her still kitchen, April could only stare, her heart thudding, her thoughts forming slowly.

Evidently he had deemed her crazy and was running for the hills. She couldn't even blame him.

Watching as he closed the door behind him, she expected him to continue walking away. She felt a little sad about that, but he turned on the top step and knocked three times in quick succession.

Understanding dawned, and with it something sweet bloomed in the middle of the mayhem that filled her chest. That sweetness spread until her heart finally settled into its rightful place beneath her breastbone, beating a more even rhythm.

She'd heard of do-overs. She was about to experience her first one.

She opened the door and once again found Cole standing on the top step. One corner of his mouth was lifted in a small smile. It was the first smile he'd ever given her, and it was beguiling.

Folding her arms, she heaved a sigh. "I wouldn't blame you if you ran. I'm a basket case," she said.

He made a sound through his pursed lips that spoke volumes. And then, holding her gaze, he said, "I'm Cole Cavanaugh."

She got lost for a moment in his brown eyes.

"I beg your pardon? What's that you said? You're April Avery? It's nice to meet you, April." He paused again. "Feel free to speak louder whenever you're ready. It sounded as though you said you could use a friend. I'd like that, too."

She didn't know whether to sniffle or smile, and wound up doing both. "You want to be my friend?" she said.

"Are you asking?" he said.

Then and there, she learned something about Cole Cavanaugh. Her sister, Marilee, would have said he was a wise guy. April agreed. Cole also happened to be among that rare breed of men known as heroes. She supposed that made him a wise guy hero. It wasn't an unattractive combination. He wasn't an unattractive man. In fact, he was one of the most attractive men she'd ever met, and it went deeper than flesh and bone.

"I guess I am asking," she said.

"Friends," he said, holding out his hand for a hand-shake.

"Yes," she agreed. She placed her hand in his. As his fingers engulfed hers, she felt a little thrum and an unexplainable connection. Her heart fluttered up into her throat again. Now it didn't scare her, for they had an understanding.

They were friends.

He carried his laptop to the table and she started a pot of coffee. Since there was no time to don contacts, she ran to her bedroom and took her glasses from their case in the drawer in her nightstand. Back in the kitchen, she poured two cups of coffee and carried them both to the table where she lowered into a chair.

He was busily opening some program or other, his eyes on the screen. It awarded her an opportunity to study him.

He had an angular face, a straight nose, dark brows and darker eyelashes. There was a faint tiny white scar above his upper lip she hadn't noticed before. She wondered if he'd gotten it in a fight or from something as innocent as falling on the playground when he was a child.

He glanced up. Finding her looking at him, he said, "Anything wrong?"

She shook her head before taking a sip of her coffee. It was true that she felt a stirring of interest to know more about him, but she didn't have to know everything today. Now that they were friends, she could take her time in that regard.

He brought up the 3-D rendering of the new floor plan he'd surely worked on most of the night, and they both turned their attention to the renovation project. Leaning forward, her elbows on the table, she studied the computer screen. The plan had been completely revised and now contained two nearly identical bedrooms where there had been one enormous master suite. A large bathroom connected the two bedrooms.

He'd thought of every detail from floors to ceilings, closets to bath fixtures. She wondered how long he'd worked on this last night. "You couldn't have gotten a lot of sleep, either."

He shook his head, but in what she was coming to recognize as his nature, no more information was forthcoming. "What do you think?" he said instead. "Is this what you had in mind for Grace's and Violet's bedrooms?"

There was no reason on God's green earth for her to suddenly need to blink away tears. Except this wasn't the way she and Jay had dreamed the upstairs would be one day. Sadly Jay wasn't here, and she needed to be strong and build a future for their children by herself now. These bedrooms with their sloping ceilings, wide plank floors, dormer windows and ample closets, along with an enormous bathroom with two sinks and heated floors, were going to be perfect for Grace and Violet as they grew up.

"April?"

She looked at Cole, and realized he'd asked her a question. "Pardon me?" she said.

"Would you like to take a few days to look this over?"

"No, thanks. I don't need a few days. I love the new design. What's next?"

"Next, I'll measure again to be certain I have the dimensions correct. After I review the materials list, I'll go down to the zoning office and pull permits, and then

I'll order materials. I need to touch base with my partner in Rochester about a project back home, and then I'll order a dumpster to be delivered here for debris. As soon as I have the proper permits and the materials, I'll be ready to begin."

"There must be something for me to sign."

He nodded. "I'll print an agreement for both of us to sign if you wish."

"How long do you expect it will take you to finish the project?" she asked.

"Four weeks. A little less if the subcontractors Riley Merrick recommended can fit us into their schedules between other jobs. It seems he has pull in the area."

She asked several questions about the plan, the bathroom, closets and paint versus stain, and he brought up several pictures of bathtubs and vanities and tiles and lighting fixtures on his computer. After she'd chosen her favorites, he closed his laptop and asked if she had any more questions.

"I can't think of any."

He went upstairs by himself. Sitting at the table sipping her coffee, she could hear footsteps overhead. Soon he was back again. They spoke for a few moments, but she could see he was eager to be on his way so he could get started. He was at the door when she said, "Cole?"

He turned slowly, and she found herself putting his lanky build and the way he moved to memory. "Yes?" he asked.

He wore fitted beige chinos that sat below his waist and a shirt that matched the coffee color of his hair. His watchband, belt and shoes were all worn brown leather. He was easy on her eyes. That was all there was to it.

"Do you have many women friends?" she asked.

He took his time considering his reply. "As of today, I have one. What about you?"

"I have lots of women friends."

That wasn't what he'd meant, but he laughed, and it reminded her of a car that hadn't been started in years. When it came to simple pleasures, he was out of practice.

"I'll be back sometime later today," he said. "I'm not sure what time."

He left her with a smile she wouldn't soon forget.

Expecting Gracie and Violet to wake up any minute, she stared out the window. Four weeks, she thought. That was how long Cole expected the project to take. After that, he would return to his life in New York.

Maybe during the next four weeks he would learn to laugh more readily. And maybe she would discover that the thought of him leaving didn't dim the light illuminating her way out of the dark tunnel she'd been in these past fourteen months. More than anything, maybe she would realize the idea she'd already fallen a little in love with him was just a dream she'd wake up from.

Because falling in love with Cole Cavanaugh was a heartache waiting to happen. She felt it to the tips of her toes.

On Monday Cole procured the proper permits and ordered materials. On Tuesday he oversaw the delivery of the dumpster and lumber and other building supplies. After that he tore out the old insulation and threw it out the upstairs window and into the waiting trash receptacle below.

The physical labor had been good for him, and he'd fallen asleep early last night, only to awaken with a jolt before 3:00 a.m. It wasn't a dream that had awakened him. It was desire for April.

And that was strictly out of the question. They'd re-established their relationship as friends. And he'd promised himself he wouldn't so much as attempt to take Jay's place in her heart or in her life.

He'd stared at the ceiling, tossed and turned, willed himself to go back to sleep, tried reading, tried watching TV. Now, at long last, it was Wednesday morning. The sun was up, birds were singing, and everywhere, people were starting their day. Leaving his truck idling at the curb in front of April's house, he drove a stake into her front yard and stapled the proper work permit to it. Returning to his truck, he pulled into the driveway and parked behind the waiting stack of lumber.

Early in his career he'd built decks and roofs and later, additions and, eventually, entire houses with a small crew and his own two hands. Gradually, he and Grant had employed their own subcontractors, skilled craftsmen who did rough-in and finish carpentry. He'd already contacted subs for the electrical, plumbing and flooring on April's remodel. Still, he would be doing much of the physical labor himself, and it was going to feel good to be building again, to be creating something lasting by the sweat of his brow and the strength of his hands.

Leaving the windows down, he got out of his truck and started for the side door. Mouthwatering aromas greeted him before he was halfway to the house.

He knocked on the screen door and heard April call, "It's open, Cole. Come on in."

Alone in the kitchen, he saw the pan of breakfast casserole and cinnamon rolls first and the coffee second. He was taking his first sip of freshly brewed coffee when his gaze landed on the table where four places had been set, as if for a family. Yearning welled inside him. He scalded his tongue and swore under his breath.

Another cup of coffee steamed from one place setting, a pink lip print on the rim. He was about to put his coffee cup down and get to work, but a movement out of the corner of his eye drew his attention to the doorway where Gracie and Violet hovered.

"How do you two take your coffee?" he said. "Black or with cream and sugar?"

Violet giggled behind her hand. "We can't have coffee, silly. We're four."

"We're almost five," Gracie corrected.

"That so?" he said, hoping his tone was cajoling. "When is your birthday?"

She skewed her little bow mouth to one side in concentration. "It's the same day as Violet's," she answered cleverly.

He laughed. And although it sounded as creaky as old door hinges, it felt good.

Just then, April bustled into the kitchen. "Good morning," she called. "I see you found the coffee."

She handed him a signed copy of the agreement he'd drawn up. Smiling at him with her eyes, she took a sip from her own mug and set it back down again. "Breakfast is ready," she said.

If the delicious-smelling cinnamon rolls and breakfast casserole cooling on top of the stove and the bowl of fresh fruit on the table was an accurate indicator, she'd been up for hours. She wasn't wearing glasses this morning and had secured her hair high on the back of her head in some sort of loose knot. Already several tendrils had escaped to wave freely around her face and collar. She wore a white summer top and a skirt in swirling shades of gray, and moved with the economy of motion of those born with the ability to do a dozen things at once.

Gracie and Violet scrambled onto their chairs, but Cole didn't move. Smiling again, April said, "Go ahead and have a seat."

"Nothing for me." He must have spoken gruffly, because even the twins looked up at him.

"You've already eaten?" April asked, two lines forming between her eyes.

He'd had a protein bar at five, but that wasn't the point. He just couldn't let himself sit in Jay's seat. There wasn't anything he could do about his desire for her. He'd promised not to get romantically involved with her, and there was something inherently intimate about sharing breakfast.

Casting a pointed glance at the fourth place setting at the table, he said, "I have equipment to unload from the truck."

With that, he turned on his heel and walked out the door. Taking a deep calming breath of fresh August air, he opened the back of his truck and dragged a heavy power saw to the tailgate.

Hefting it into his arms, he turned and swore softly, for he almost ran headlong into April. She squinted up at him in the dappled shade, but she held her ground, her arms folded stubbornly, her chin raised.

"What?" he said.

She rolled her eyes. "You stole my line."

He set the heavy saw back on the tailgate. Now that

his hands were free, they wound up on his hips. "I have work to do, April."

"I can see that. But now that we've become friends and all," she said sarcastically, "maybe you would care to tell me what I did to thoroughly tick you off."

"You didn't do anything."

"Then what is it?"

"You don't need to feed me, that's all."

"I feed all my friends. Ask them if you don't believe me." She looked at him as if daring him to tell her what had gotten his back up.

When a retired couple walking their dog called, "Good morning, April," she waved good-naturedly. Obviously, she was only mad at him, not the world.

"Do you seat all your friends in Jay's place, too?" he asked.

She moved as if thrust backward by a strong gust of wind. The look in her eyes made him feel like something he stepped in.

"We don't have assigned seats," she said. "We never have."

His vehemence drained out of him like air from a leaky valve. He'd overreacted, which was the mother of all understatements. Promise or no promise, it wasn't going to be easy to maintain a friendship when he wanted so much more. Running a hand down his face, he studied her.

Her eyes were wide-open and golden brown, her cheeks pink, her sleeveless shirt white and summery and feminine. She looked pretty and dewy. And hurt. He owed her an explanation and an apology. He'd never been good at asking for forgiveness. It ranked right up there with ramming a rusty nail through his hand.

In a voice he barely recognized, he said, "Before Jay died, I had a dream."

She watched him closely. "A nightmare?"

He nodded. "I was awake a lot last night." There was no sense telling her the reason he'd awakened at three. "I had a nightmare, but I thought a lot about Jay, too."

"And did your dream have something to do with Jay?"

"It has me feeling off this morning. I'm sorry."

Shading her eyes with one hand, she looked up at him. "I find it interesting neither of us slept well last night. Maybe the next time will be better. We're some pair, aren't we?"

He had nothing to say to that.

"Except we're not a pair, are we?" she asked.

This time he shook his head.

"But we are friends." He didn't know why she stumbled on the wording, but she continued. "And like my other friends, you're welcome to the food I prepare these next four weeks. I enjoy cooking and I love to bake. You don't need to ask or wait for me to offer. It brings me pleasure to know my friends enjoy my culinary creations."

She started away from him. Speaking over her shoulder, she said, "Just help yourself. Feel free to eat at the table, in your truck or standing on your head."

With a lift of her chin that had humph written all over it, she walked regally toward the house. Cole stood in the dappled shade of an enormous maple tree and watched until she disappeared inside.

The door bounced shut, bringing the morning's misunderstanding to a close. The sun was already hot and the humidity was rising fast. It was going to be another scorcher. He unloaded his saws and power tools, donned his favorite tool belt and set up the sawhorses near the stack of lumber in the driveway. All the while he pictured himself standing on his head.

He hadn't done that in years. He honestly doubted if he could now, but the thought of it made him feel young, almost carefree.

Or perhaps April should get the credit for that.

Chapter Seven

Other than catching a glimpse of April pushing Gracie and Violet on the swings, Cole didn't see her again the rest of Wednesday morning. From time to time he heard the twins laughing, and at one point he smelled something mouthwatering and sweet. Around noon the garage door went up and then down.

When he made a pass through the kitchen on his way outside for more supplies, the house was utterly quiet. April and the girls must have gone out. There was a pan of something cooling on the counter. Next to it was a small gleaming plate, knife and fork.

Back upstairs, he tuned an old radio to a local station and concentrated on his work. By three o'clock he'd insulated the entire ceiling and had started on one wall.

Gracie and Violet were playing outside the next time he went down for more insulation. After hefting a cumbersome roll onto one shoulder, he turned around and saw April walking toward him, a tall glass in each hand.

Wearing blue today, she stopped directly in his path and said, "I noticed you found a slice of caramel apple coffee cake."

"Actually, I found two slices," he admitted a little sheepishly as he lowered the bundle back to the ground.

Careful not to touch her fingers, he took the glass she held out to him, but he couldn't seem to refrain from looking at her mouth as she sipped her lemonade. What was there about her that instilled this sense of urgency and yearning for something he couldn't even name? Whatever it was, he'd felt it from the other side of the world before he'd even met her.

"What's your favorite color?"

He started. "Pardon me?"

"Your favorite color. I was just wondering what it is."

He sipped his beverage but made no reply.

"I already know you have a penchant for sweets. You washed the plate and fork you used, so I think it's safe to say you're well mannered. What's your favorite kind of movie?"

"I haven't seen a movie in years."

"Remind me to never watch the Oscars with you. What about music?"

"What are you doing?" he asked.

"Besides helping you take a break and have something to drink so you don't pass out from heatstroke and dehydration, you mean? Short term, I'm trying to fill an awkward silence. The bigger picture is that you're remodeling my upstairs and will be here for the next four weeks. Which means we'll be in close proximity. Plus, I like to get to know my friends."

"Are you always such a smart aleck?" he said.

She laughed. "Always. Well?"

On a groan, he said, "I haven't thought about my favorite anything in a long time. I don't have a favorite color."

"Everyone has a favorite color. Violet's is purple and Gracie's is pink. Jay's was green. My dad's was blue. My sister, Marilee's, is black. If you ever meet her, it'll make perfect sense."

She took another sip of her drink, and he couldn't stop his gaze from straying to her mouth again.

"As I said, everyone has one. My friend Lacey's is turquoise."

"The peacock?" he asked before he could stop himself.

She reacted with mild surprise. "Lacey reminds you of a peacock?"

"I happen to associate people with animals. It isn't intentional."

She looked fascinated. "It's automatic then?"

"I suppose."

"What is Gracie?"

"A unicorn."

Both their gazes went to the backyard where her darling little unicorn was trying to pry a plastic watering can out of her sister's hands. "Give it back!" she yelled, scrambling for it.

"It's mine!" Violet screeched, trying to break free of Gracie's hold.

"I had it first," Gracie insisted.

The yelling quickly escalated into ear-piercing screaming. "A unicorn," April said, unfazed. "I can see that. What is Violet?"

"A dragonfly," he said, although right now they were both leaning more toward banshees. "Are you going to do something about their squabble?"

"I'm going to give them another minute to work it out."

As they watched, Gracie wrangled the watering can out of her sister's hands, which produced another ear-piercing screech from Violet, followed by, "It's mine!"

"You can't take stuff away from people," Gracie yelled back. "It's a rule."

"You're not the boss of me!" Violet retorted.

Now that she had it in her possession again, Gracie looked the watering can over then promptly handed it back, proving she hadn't really wanted it; she'd just wanted to be right. "Wanna play princess?" she asked.

Violet pouted for good measure then dropped the watering can and followed the path her sister took to the playhouse Jay built the summer before he left for the war. He'd gone into great detail in his description of the structure when they'd been stationed together. Now that Cole saw the peaked roof and the gingerbread trim, the little windows with their moveable shutters and window boxes, and the tiny front porch, he understood his friend's pride.

"Do they do that often?" he asked.

"What? Fight? Not as much as my sister and I used to. Did you fight with your siblings?"

"I was an only child," he said. "Until my mom got cancer, we moved around a lot for my father's job. As the new kid, I was in observer mode a lot."

"Is that when you started associating people with animals?" April asked.

He hadn't thought about it, but perhaps that was how it had begun.

"Do you associate everyone you meet with some sort of animal?" she asked, undeniably curious.

"Not everyone. Some people."

"People you met at the party the other night?"

He shrugged and followed her gaze to a yard behind hers where her brother-in-law Will was filling a wading pool for his kids.

"If Will Avery were an animal, what would he be?" she asked.

"A dolphin," Cole said without having to think about it.

April's mouth formed a perfect O. "Will is intelligent, communicative, friendly and playful. He would be a great dolphin. What are some of the others you met at the cookout?" she asked.

Cole didn't know how they'd come to be talking about this, but he replied, "There was the walking stick."

"You mean like the insect?"

At his nod, he could see her rifling through her guest list in her mind, and knew the moment she came to her neighbor, for she glanced at the house visible over the hedge. "Bernadette Fletcher is my quietest neighbor. She's nearly six feet tall, and yet she somehow makes herself invisible in a crowd. Amazing."

"I'd appreciate it if you kept that little jewel to yourself," he said. "I'm not sure she'd find the comparison flattering, though from my perspective it's always a compliment."

April rubbed her hands together and smiled, and Cole knew her compliance was going to come at a price.

"I won't mention it on one condition. Tell me at least three more."

"Whose do you want to know?" he asked, dragging his gaze from her mouth. Again.

April considered the possibilities. She'd never heard of anyone, besides her, who made associations like this. Ever since she was a child she'd perceived people as scents and seasons. Gracie was the first daisy to bloom every summer and Violet was homemade strawberry ice cream on the Fourth of July. Although April wanted to know which animal Cole associated with *every* person he'd met at the party, she started with one of the more colorful and perhaps most misunderstood people she knew.

"Which animal would Noah Sullivan be?" she asked.

"He's the pilot, right?" At her nod, he said, "One of the Shackleford horses."

Oh my goodness, yes, April thought as she pictured the famous horses running wild and free on the Outer Banks of North Carolina. "What is my sister-in-law, Gabby?"

"Is she the strawberry blonde?" he asked.

With a nod, she explained, "From the beginning, Gabby and I clicked. She has a sixth sense about people, but she's sly about it. I'm guessing she reminds you of a red fox."

He shook his head as if to say, amateur. "A white tiger," he said.

"Hmm," April hummed, for like a white tiger, Gabby was exotic and supple and rare. In a gentle tone of voice, she asked, "What was Jay?"

Cole hesitated. Then, in a voice that had gone noticeably deeper, he said, "He was a leopard. Now I wish I would have told him that."

She swallowed a lump in her throat, for like a leopard, Jay had been sleek, strong and stealthy. There was a saying, a leopard never changed its spots. Similarly, Jay had never wavered from exactly who and what he was. "What am I?" she asked.

"*You* are keeping me from my work." He handed her his empty glass and reached for the roll of insulation at his knee. Hefting it onto his shoulder again, he said, "If you want the girls to move into their rooms before they leave for college, I need to get busy."

If April had been able to see his expression, she would have known he was smiling as he went inside with his cumbersome bundle of insulation. Oddly enough, she felt like smiling, too. Perhaps there was something to be said for finding a friend in Cole Cavanaugh.

Unfortunately, she found that something deep inside her was wishing for more.

On Friday afternoon Cole placed six two-by-fours across the sawhorses in April's driveway and carefully measured each one. The project was progressing more quickly than he'd anticipated. Of course, he hadn't anticipated unseen help. He'd planned to hire the two teenage kids across the street to carry the insulation and drywall upstairs, but when he'd arrived yesterday he'd found the remainder of the stack had already been carried upstairs. Evidently Jay's brothers had done the honors the night before. Earlier this morning Bernadette Fletcher's husband, Neil, had *happened* to stop by and had helped Cole raise a wall.

When the rooms were studded in and insulated the crew he'd hired would hang the drywall and finish it. And yet, day by day, he was coming to realize that April's door truly was always open. She hadn't been exaggerating about having many friends. Besides those he'd met at the party, he'd been introduced to a wedding planner named Chelsea, a teacher named Yvette and a reporter whose name escaped him.

Focusing on his work, he drew a line on each board at the proper measurement. Carefully double-checking each mark, he reached for the saw.

There was a light tap on his shoulder. He jumped straight up. Swinging around, he found April smiling apologetically.

He removed his ear protection and accepted the tall glass she handed to him. "It's that time already?"

She nodded, for this was the third day in a row she'd brought him something cold to drink at shortly after three. "What is Jay's father?" she asked as he tipped up his glass of sweet peach iced tea.

Each day the beverage was a different flavor, and each day she pressed him for more animal associations. Yesterday, she'd asked about Jay's mother, who reminded Cole of a swan, and Jay's sister, Elizabeth, whom Cole perceived as a cockatoo, and the wedding planner, who was as beautiful and aloof as a Balinese cat. Wearing faded jeans, a sleeveless yellow top and a bracelet made out of turquoise, April patiently sipped her iced tea while she waited for him to answer her question about Jay's father.

"A golden eagle," he said in a matter-of-fact tone.

He was coming to expect her gaze to stray to some far-off place over his shoulder as she contemplated each association. "I can see that," she eventually said on a smile identical to the one he'd pictured before falling asleep last night.

"What about Regan?" she said.

It took him a few seconds to remember which of Jay's sisters was Regan. "A zebra."

She never tried to hide her surprise and he never tired of witnessing the smile that spread across her face when she'd made sense of his comparison. "I read that no two zebras have identical stripes."

"I read that, too," he said.

"Then you see her as an exotic and unique member of her herd."

"You're the one who puts it into words."

"And what am I?" she asked.

Cole wasn't going to answer, and he was pretty sure she knew it. She watched him closely, but didn't ask him again. She smiled, and he believed she enjoyed these afternoon breaks as much as he did. The only negative he could think of was that another day was passing. And his time here in Orchard Hill was one more day shorter. She folded her arms and tapped one foot in obvious waiting. "Which animal, pray tell, am I?"

He smiled to himself because he'd known she wouldn't let this one go. He could have told her which animal she reminded him of, but he wasn't going to, at least not today. The time wasn't right yet.

It only seemed to make her more curious. "Please tell me you don't see me as a snake or a rat or some slimy horrible creature."

"None of the above," he said with a slow grin that was coming far easier these days. He drained the remainder of his beverage, and with a sincere thank you, he went to his truck to retrieve his phone so he could call the plumber and electrician back. If he was a man prone to whistling he probably would have been whistling some nameless tune.

Friendship with April Avery felt good.

April started for the house, watching Cole as she went. It seemed to her his gait was getting easier. It seemed to her that he enjoyed their daily breaks. She certainly enjoyed them. She gained a little more insight into Cole's history and his personality every day. For instance, she'd learned that he'd turned thirty-four in June, and was now slightly older than Jay would ever be. He'd lost his mother to leukemia when he was a child and his father to an aneurysm ten years later. He'd been in one bar fight and had never been arrested or audited by the IRS. Once, when he was ten, he'd fainted from the sight of his own blood. Some of it she'd learned from the background check she'd had run before she'd hired Cole, but she never tired of hearing it in his own words. There was so much more she wanted to know, but today was only Friday. He would be here at least three more weeks.

She stopped in midstride. If the fact that there was a limited time frame on their association gave her pause, it wasn't his fault. It wasn't his fault that every day she found herself studying his face, feature by feature, putting it to memory, to be taken out after the girls were fast asleep, either. The truth was, her heart sped up when she heard his car door slam at one minute after eight every morning. She liked him. She liked all her friends. But not like this. She was trying to decide what she was going to do about it.

She carried their glasses inside, and told herself she didn't have to decide what do about her burgeoning feelings for Cole today. He would be here at least three more weeks. Suddenly three more weeks did not seem like much time at all.

Through the kitchen door she watched as Gracie and Violet made their way carefully toward her across the backyard. They'd dressed alike today in tangerine shorts and ruffled shirts tied at the back of their necks. Both cradled something in their arms.

Heading outside to see what they were up to, she waited at the edge of the patio. "Look, Mama," Violet called. "Just what I always wanted."

They sidled closer, and April saw that they each held an unbelievably tiny gray rabbit in the crooks of their little arms. "There's two," Gracie explained patiently. "One for Violet and one for me."

"I've been praying and praying for a puppy. God musta heard me, 'cause a bunny's almost as good," Violet declared excitedly.

Oh, dear.

April knelt down on her knees. "They are adorable," she said, gently touching a finger to the little head of first one bunny and then the other. "Where did you find them?"

"Under the Daddy Tree," Gracie answered guilelessly.

April didn't know where they'd gotten the name for the small blue spruce Jay had planted after he'd finished their playhouse, but she loved that they called it the Daddy Tree.

Violet was giving April a guarded look. Growing

suspicious of her mother's intentions, she eased the arm nestling the bunny away.

Gracie hadn't caught on to the fact that they couldn't keep the wild rabbits. With her heart wide-open, she said, "They were sleeping in a nest made out of grass. We never saw rabbits so little."

"And did you see their mother rabbit nearby?" April asked.

Her little girl's eyes widened, but she didn't reply, which was answer enough.

"They're ours now," Violet stated. As if she had no intention of broaching any argument from her mother, she hurried to add, "I named mine Bitsy and Gracie's is Fluffy."

"Those are fine names," April said, noticing that Cole was off his phone now and was coming this way. "I'm sure their mother will appreciate your assistance in naming her children when we take them back to their nest."

"I'm not bringin' mine back," Violet said.

"Honey, they're too little to leave their mother. They'll get sick if we keep them from her."

Cole reached the patio as the first tears were forming in Violet's eyes. He leaned down. There was sawdust on his jeans and patience in the depths of his brown eyes. "What we have here," he said matter-of-factly, "are newborn garden rabbits. You two must be extra special because mother rabbits don't usually allow humans to see their babies when they're this new."

"They don't?" Gracie asked with innocent wonder.

He shook his head earnestly.

April watched her daughters responding to Cole.

Young and utterly vulnerable, they looked at him with such trust.

They'd been beyond excited when she'd taken them school shopping yesterday, but today their chins were down, and their eyes sad, their little hearts breaking. They yearned for a puppy, but puppies required companionship and constant supervision and energy and April was going back to teaching after Labor Day and just didn't know how she could possibly handle one more responsibility.

"Their mother is probably watching you from her secret hiding place to make sure you're being gentle with her babies," Cole said. "She won't mind if you hold them for another minute or two. Then you need to put them back in their nest so she can feed them milk."

"We have milk in the fridge." Violet wasn't giving up.

"The milk in your refrigerator comes from cows," Cole explained. "Cow milk would make rabbits this small very sick, so sick they might die."

"Uh-uh," Gracie said.

"It would?" A tear ran down Violet's cheek as she turned to her mother for confirmation.

Tears threatened April's eyes, too. Nodding gravely, she could see the battle raging within her curly-haired daughter between doing what she wanted more than anything and doing what the rabbits needed to stay alive.

Her little girls had experienced tragic loss. They'd been affected by death in ways children this young should never be.

"We'll go to the store and get the kind of milk they drink then," Gracie insisted.

"They drink rabbit milk," Cole explained. "And only mother rabbits have it. You don't want them to get sick, do you?"

Both girls seemed to know it wasn't a question.

The bunnies were starting to wiggle. "They're hungry and afraid," April said gently. "They want their mother just like you do when you're afraid."

"We have to take them back to their nest now so their mother can feed them," Cole stated.

The twins communicated silently with each other with a look. Violet nodded first. With a sigh bigger than she was, Gracie surrendered, too. Utterly forlorn, they fell into step between April and Cole.

The four of them made their way slowly across the backyard, stopping before the Daddy Tree, which was taller than the twins now. Lowering to his knees, Cole held the branches back where Gracie pointed, and April gently placed first Gracie's and then Violet's little charge into the nest the mother rabbit had lined with her own soft fur.

Tears ran unchecked down both girls' faces. April would give anything to be able to protect them from life's sadness and disappointments.

"I'll bet their mother won't mind if we look in on them every morning," Cole told the girls.

"Every morning?" Violet asked on a sniffle.

"I think the bunnies would like that," April whispered. "Let's tell them goodbye for now so their mama can come out of her hiding place and feed her hungry children. We'll come back to see them tomorrow."

"Bye, Fluffy."

"Bye, Bitsy. See you in the morning."

Cole lowered the spruce bow back into place and rose

stiffly to his feet. Holding hands, the girls followed the adults slowly, and April mouthed a thank-you to Cole.

"Catastrophe avoided," he said, surprising her when he reached out and brushed the tear from her face. Without another word, he returned to his stack of lumber and power tools as if everything was back to normal.

All around April, everything truly did appear to be normal. A robin splashed in the birdbath and her nephews screeched from their wading pool. A ray of sunshine poked through a cloud overhead, and Gracie and Violet swooped down to pick dandelions.

Cole had touched her, one finger brushing gently, innocently across her cheek. He'd touched her, and it wasn't like the other night when they'd kissed. His brief touch today was different. And it had changed something deep inside her.

Following her daughters back inside, April put each facet of this interlude to memory. She would take it out later and examine every layer. And she would recall the moment she'd fallen the rest of the way in love.

She hadn't wanted to fall in love again. She certainly hadn't intended to fall in love with a man with deep emotional scars of his own.

But it was done. She loved Cole.

Please, God, she thought. *Let him love me back.*

It takes a village to raise a child.

Looking around her patio table where she and her closest friends had gathered on this sunny Saturday afternoon, April thought there should be an equally profound statement for girlfriends, for she didn't know how she would have survived this past year without the three women sitting with her today.

"Do you know what Noah did last night?" Lacey Sullivan asked.

"Do I need to cover Joey's ears?" Julia Sullivan asked quietly so as not to wake her toddler son who was napping in her arms.

Chelsea Reynolds shuddered. "I'm not sure I want to know what he did. Men can be such jerks."

"He painted my toenails," Lacey said, smiling dreamily. "I can't see my toes anymore, which was what I was telling him after my shower. And what did he do? He helped me into one of the new rocking chairs we bought for the nursery, and then he painted all ten of my toenails pink, for our baby girls, he said."

Everyone peered under the table at her pretty pink toes. "Would you stop?" Chelsea grumbled. With her fork poised over her slice of peach pie, she said, "I'm trying to hate all men over here and you're not making it easy."

Of the three women sitting with her today, April had known Lacey the longest. Raised in the small apartment over the town's seediest bar, Lacey had grown up with a chip on her shoulder and an ability to take care of herself. April secretly considered the sassy, smart expectant mother her best friend.

She thought the world of Chelsea, too. Dark-haired and gorgeous, she was an extremely popular wedding planner. Having just come from being propositioned by the groom himself following the ceremony of an opulent wedding she'd meticulously planned, Chelsea had good reason to distrust the opposite sex. Only her closest friends knew she secretly longed to find an honorable man.

Of the three friends gathered with her today, April

had known Julia Sullivan the least amount of time, for she'd only been in Orchard Hill for a year. Her latest round of chemo had made her hair fall out. Again. Today she wore a blue scarf that matched her eyes, but on the day she'd returned to Orchard Hill last summer, she'd worn a floppy hat to hide her baldness.

Before they met her, a lot of people in Orchard Hill had judged her harshly for leaving her newborn son on his father's doorstep shortly after his birth. But they hadn't known that the delicate watercolor artist with the lilting Southern accent had been fighting for her life back in North Carolina while also raising her teenage half sister, Annalise.

Julia had been beyond shocked when she'd discovered she was pregnant following an idyllic vacation romance the summer before last. From the beginning, the pregnancy had been plagued with complications, and then, when she was nearly four months along she'd learned she had breast cancer. Her chance for survival lessened with every month she failed to seek treatment, treatment that meant she had to choose between her chances and her child's.

Her love for her baby had been instant and fierce. Somehow, she knew her son would be a fighter like her. She underwent surgery to remove the tumor from her breast, but would wait until after her baby was born to begin chemotherapy and radiation treatment.

Like her pregnancy, her labor and delivery had been fraught with complications. Her baby was born a month prematurely. As soon as she and the baby were strong enough, she'd secretly brought Joey to his father's doorstep then waited at the edge of the orchard until she was certain he'd taken their son inside. With tears streaming down her face, she returned to North Carolina to begin the rigorous treatment, hoping and praying she might live long enough to raise her child.

The minute she was able, she came back for baby Joseph, arriving shortly after Jay had died. Julia had been going through her own hell on earth, and yet she'd reached out to April in her darkest hour. Each had found a kindred spirit in the other.

Marsh had convinced Julia to marry him, and for a time it had seemed as though they might live happily ever after. But three months ago her cancer reared again, this time in her other breast. She'd had more surgery, more radiation and even more grueling chemotherapy treatment.

Sitting across from April today, Julia kept a protective hand on Joey's back. Her skin looked ghostly pale against Joey's rosy complexion. April reminded herself that Julia was in remission. Her lymph nodes hadn't been affected and her prognosis was good, and yet sometimes she saw something in those wizened blue eyes that sent worry to the pit of her stomach. Not today, though. Today, the four of them were enjoying peach pie, iced tea and one another.

In a series of small, ungainly motions, Lacey rose to her feet. "Another trip to the bathroom?" Chelsea exclaimed.

"It's crowded in here," Lacey said, her hand resting protectively on her bulging belly. "This has been going on day and night. There are a hundred reasons I cannot wait to have these babies. I want to hold them, kiss them, nurse them, care for them, marvel at them. Right now all I can think about is having them so I can sleep."

Julia caught April's eye and winked. Even Chelsea,

who was single and had limited experience with children, knew that having twins wasn't exactly a relaxing experience.

It was a warm, sunny Saturday afternoon. Other than the occasional humming noise eighteen-month-old Joey made in his sleep, the only sounds April had heard for the past half hour were Gracie, Violet and the neighborhood children playing in the wading pool in their cousin's backyard, her friends' laughter and the pounding of Cole's hammer carrying through the window upstairs.

Moving slowly these days, Lacey finally reached the door. "Chelsea insists chivalry is dead," April heard her say. "Do you want to tell her she's wrong or shall I?"

April wasn't surprised to see Cole holding the door for Lacey, but she doubted anybody was more shocked than him when she planted a kiss on his cheek on her way by. "That," Lacey said, "is for seeing me as a peacock and not a beached whale."

April's gaze flew to his. Watching him walk toward her, she said, "I hope you don't mind that I told her. She feels bigger than a barn and I was trying to cheer her up."

"Did it help?" he asked.

"You're the one she kissed. You tell me."

April smiled.

And he almost did.

"Have you told all your friends?" he asked.

"Only Lacey."

"Did she tell us what?" Chelsea asked.

Cole finally acknowledged the other two women at the table. "April discovered a peculiarity I have for seeing animal traits in people."

"Has April mentioned that she perceives Lacey as spiced apple cider on a crisp autumn night?"

He shook his head, and April pulled a face at Chelsea. "Thanks a lot."

"I didn't know it was a secret," Chelsea replied.

"Is it a secret?" Cole asked April.

She shook her head. And he asked, "What are your friends?"

"Chelsea is a field of lavender in May and Julia is an ocean breeze at dawn's early light."

"What am I?" he asked.

"Nice try," she said. "Tell me which animal I remind you of and we'll talk." She laughed, and there was such joy in it that even Lacey, who was gingerly making her way back to the table, looked at April peculiarly.

"What's going on?" she asked, lowering carefully into her empty chair.

But April didn't hear.

"Did Gracie and Violet visit the rabbits this morning?" he asked April.

"They were up *very* early to do just that, but I made them wait until it was light outside," she said.

He smiled, and it did something to her heartbeat.

"Maybe we should have told them they could look in on the rabbits before bedtime instead of in the morning," he said.

"Hindsight."

This time they both smiled.

On the other side of the table, Chelsea held her hand in front of Lacey's face. "Can you see my fingers?" she asked.

"Uh, Chelsea? I'm pregnant not blind."

"Then we're not invisible," Chelsea said, tipping her head toward April and Cole.

"Ahh," Lacey said as understanding dawned.

Temporarily oblivious to the others at the table, April watched Cole stride to his truck parked in the driveway. She was convinced his gait was getting smoother. He wore jeans and a black T-shirt, his tool belt riding low on his hips. He rummaged through a large stainless steel tool chest, the action drawing attention to the corded muscles in his back, shoulders and arms.

Watching, too, Chelsea toyed with her bracelets; Julia softly patted Joey's little back and Lacey gently massaged her taut belly. Only April's hand came to rest over her fluttering heart.

Glancing at the time on her phone, Chelsea rose to her feet, and with a sigh, quietly said, "I'd love to stay and watch the show, but I have a six-course wedding dinner and an elegant reception to attend to, even if the groom is a sack of dog poop."

"Will you tell the bride?" Julia asked.

"If he'd propositioned me before the ceremony I might have tried to broach the subject with the bride. What good would it do now? The music and the flowers and the dresses and the vows and a hundred other details turned out perfectly. It took us a year and a half to plan this wedding. I give the marriage six months at the most."

She pointed a purple-tipped fingernail at Lacey and said, "Do not go into labor." To Julia, "Do not go out of remission." And to April, "I'll talk to you tomorrow."

With that, Chelsea sashayed to her car. April saw her say something to Cole as she passed him. After she was out of his sight, she turned and looked back at the three women sitting at the table. With a wink, she held both hands out, palm-side up, and mouthed, "Nothin'." She wasn't accustomed to being ignored by the opposite sex.

Lacey and Julia looked at one another the way Violet and Gracie often did, communicating silently. "What is it?" April asked.

With a loud clank, Cole closed the lid of the tool chest. Lacey waited until he'd ambled into the house before she turned to her best friend and smirked the way she had when she'd been a cocky teenager growing up over the town's seediest bar.

"What is it?" April prodded again.

"It's nothing," Lacey said.

"I know you," April said quietly. "When you have that look in your eye and that knowing grin on your face it's never nothing."

"Okay, you asked for it. What's going on between you and the sexy war hero with the haunted look in his eyes and to-die-for physique?"

"Nothing's going on," April whispered.

"Oh, sugar, something's going on. You two couldn't take your eyes off one another just now. If I wasn't madly in love with Noah, I'd have a serious crush on Cole, too."

"If only it were just a crush," April said.

Lacey's mouth gaped. "It's more than that?" she asked.

April couldn't help noticing that Julia remained silent. "He's been here less than two weeks and I feel like I'm falling in love. I know it's only been fourteen months since Jay died. I know I wasn't ready. But I can't seem to help myself."

Leaning forward as far as the twins she was carrying would allow, Lacey whispered, "How in love?"

Leave it to Lacey to get right to the heart of the matter. "He makes my heart feel like it's doing somersaults into the pit of my stomach. Maybe it doesn't mean I'm in love."

"What then, in lust?" Lacey asked.

April gasped. "No. I mean, kinda, but I'm afraid it's more than that."

Lacey exclaimed, "That's wonderful. We're your best friends. Why haven't you told us?"

"I haven't even told him," April said. "Besides, it's completely one-sided."

"Oh, I think he knows," Lacey insisted quietly.

"He couldn't. We agreed we should be friends. That was after I threw myself into his arms and kissed him."

"I'm no expert," Lacey stated, "but isn't kissing him first and then deciding to be friends backward?"

"You think?" April agreed.

"So how was it? Kissing him, I mean."

April's sigh said it all. "We agreed friendship is better for both of us. No one can have too many friends, right? It's certainly safer, and feeling safe felt good. But then we helped Gracie and Violet put a pair of tiny baby rabbits back in their nest yesterday and I felt my heart tumble top over bottom into my stomach. It's okay. I'm not sorry. I never thought I'd feel this way again. With Jay it was mutual, you know? This is different. Cole doesn't feel the same way about me."

"Are you sure about that?" Lacey moved this way and that as she tried to get comfortable in her chair.

"I'm sure, Lace."

"I hate to be the one to tell you you're wrong, but you're wrong."

April looked at her friend. "Why do you say that?"

"You saw what happened when Chelsea just left," Lacey said. "That flawless face and those violet eyes, that gorgeous hair, that luscious body, that dress, those heels and the sway of those hips. She's the mark against which every woman within a hundred-mile radius is measured. The only man who doesn't fall at her feet is one blinded by his interest in someone else. FYI. Cole didn't give Chelsea more than a cursory good-bye just now."

April looked at Julia. For a moment she was distracted by the sad expression in her friend's blue eyes. But Lacey continued talking, and April turned her attention back to her.

"Honey, that man is interested in you."

"He's leaving as soon as he finishes the upstairs," April said.

"When will that be?" Lacey asked.

Again, April wondered why Julia had become so quiet. Joey was asleep on her shoulder, but she'd talked earlier, so she couldn't be worried that would wake him. Was she feeling all right? Perhaps she was just tired.

April couldn't help sighing as she considered Lacey's question, for Cole was working today, and it was Saturday. He was obviously in a hurry to be done and gone. "He has a life and a thriving business in upstate New York and is leaving in a few weeks."

"Then you need to make your move."

"What are you suggesting?" she whispered.

"You've already kissed him, right?" Lacey said softly. "What's your seduction style? Unbuttoning his shirt? Or unbuttoning yours? Whatever you do afterward, kissing him again would be a wonderful place to begin."

Leaving April with that bit of sage advice, Lacey lumbered to her feet. April and Julia exchanged a concerned look.

"I know. Again, right?" Lacey said. And then her eyes grew round. "Oh, no," she said on a moan.

"What's wrong?" Julia finally broke her silence.

"I think I'm having a contraction."

"You think?" Julia asked her sister-in-law.

"But your C-section is scheduled for ten days from now," April said, as if Lacey wasn't aware of that minor detail.

One hand flattened on the table, the other supporting the small of her back, Lacey said, "Tell that to these two." Then she grasped her belly with both hands and moaned. "Oh-oh," she said. "Houston, we have a problem."

No one needed to ask, for the liquid puddling at her feet was explanation enough. Lacey's water had broken. These babies were not going to wait until their scheduled C-section to be born.

Julia jumped up so fast Joey awoke with a jolt. April helped Lacey sit down then darted to the house to get a towel and her phone.

Julia stayed with Lacey, who moaned out loud, for her contractions were coming hard and fast. Very hard and very fast. Having been rudely awakened, Joey was crying, and April nearly ran headlong into Cole who was coming out as she was going in. "Call 911!" she said.

"What's happened?"

"Lacey's babies are coming."

He swore under his breath then whisked his phone from his back pocket. After what seemed like forever but was actually a matter of minutes, sirens blared in the distance. Lacey's contractions were coming with little time in between.

Hearing the commotion, Will and Kristy and all the kids came running. Joey wailed on Julia's hip. Lacey was moaning; April was talking to Lacey's doctor on her phone. Julia was talking to her husband and he was already trying to reach Noah, who was test-piloting a Piper Cherokee some five thousand feet above Orchard Hill.

On the line with the 911 dispatcher, Cole told Lacey, "The ambulance's ETA is five minutes." He listened to the person talking him through this on the phone then turned back to Lacey. "They want you to stay calm and breathe through your mouth like you were taught to do in birthing class."

"I was on bedrest then, and didn't take a birthing class. I'm supposed to have a C-section so I didn't think I needed to know how to breathe through hard labor."

April and Julia demonstrated for their friend.

Lacey doubled over in pain.

It was official. Pandemonium had erupted at 404 Baldwin Street.

And if that wasn't enough, there was no doubt in April's mind now that she was indeed in love.

Chapter Eight

The ambulance came charging into April's driveway with its lights flashing and sirens blaring. Joey stopped crying at the commotion, and Gracie and Violet started.

Three paramedics swarmed out. In seconds, they surrounded Lacey and lowered her onto a gurney. They took her vitals and did a quick oral history of pertinent information such as her age, who her doctor was, when her babies were due and when the contractions had started.

How they made sense of anything was a mystery to April, for everyone seemed to be talking at once. The paramedics were obviously accustomed to working under such conditions, for one of them, a large burly young man who looked strong enough to lift cars off people, calmed the spectators while pressing them back, thus giving Lacey a little privacy while the other two worked on their knees on either side of her. One monitored the babies' heartbeats and the other, a woman who seemed to be in charge, draped a sheet over her.

April felt helpless. Julia looked as pale as a ghost, and Will's newborn son was wailing hungrily from Kristy's arms while Will tried to draw his other two little boys and his nieces' interest to an intricate spiderweb on the arbor by the garage. The ploy had little success, for what child chose an everyday spider over flashing lights and three uniformed paramedics?

"You're at six centimeters. Let's get you to the hospital," the woman in charge said to Lacey.

She started to hyperventilate. "I want Noah!" She twisted her head around until she found April.

April rushed to her friend's side, the girls on her shirttails. "Julia talked to Marsh," April said, wincing beneath Lacey's grip. "He's already called Tom Bender," she said, referring to the owner of the airstrip north of Orchard Hill. "Tom radioed Noah. Your husband is coming in for a landing as we speak. He'll be at the hospital shortly after we get there. You're going to meet your babies soon, Lacey. Think about that. Two healthy baby girls who might look like you and have personalities as wild and free as Noah's."

"Are you trying to scare me or make me feel better?" Lacey asked. But the distraction worked, and she smiled, for a moment at least.

The paramedics secured Lacey to the gurney, and then lifted her into the ambulance. Suddenly Julia wasn't the only one looking as pale as a sheet. "Come with me?" Lacey whispered.

April nodded. Turning, she searched the small crowd, which now included neighbors, too. Julia, who had spent far too much time in hospitals this past year and a half said, "I'll grab Joey's diaper bag and meet you there."

"We'll keep the girls with us until you get back," Kristy told April.

"No!" Gracie and Violet wailed.

"It's okay," April crooned to her daughters. "Mama is going to ride in the ambulance with Auntie Lacey. I'll tell you all about my adventure when I get home. Soon there will be two more twin girls for us to visit. For now you can play with Garret and Tyler at Uncle Will and Aunt Kristy's."

"Noooo! We wanna come, too."

"Girls, come with us," Kristy said.

"We wanna go with Mama."

Out of the clear blue came Cole's deep, steady voice. "What if they stay here with me?" Cole said.

Everyone except Lacey and the paramedics looked at Cole. He hunkered down at eye level with Gracie and Violet, and then he said, "We'll look in on the rabbits again just to make sure their mother is feeding them enough. Later we'll draw chalk lines on the floors upstairs so you can see exactly where your new doorways, closets and everything in the bathroom will be."

The girls stared into his eyes as if determining something vital. After a few seconds, Violet turned toward her mother and said, "Are you coming back, Mama?"

Miracles of miracles, they'd stopped crying, though April nearly started in herself. Her daughters had few memories of their father anymore, but they remembered that he'd promised he would return. It was a promise he'd been unable to keep.

"Of course she's coming back," Cole declared. "The hospital is what, eight blocks away? Your aunt Lacey will rest there for a few days with her babies but they won't let your mom stay."

It was settled. Gracie and Violet would stay here with Cole. And their mother would return to them as soon as Lacey's babies were born.

"Bye, Mama!"

"Bye, sweet peas."

She glanced up at Cole.

"I'll guard them with my life," he said.

Staring into his eyes much the way Violet and Gracie had, she said, "I know you will." She hugged her daughters then climbed into the back of the ambulance. One of the paramedics immediately closed the doors. Looking through the glass, April waved to Violet and Gracie, who stood on either side of Cole, each of them holding one of his hands. He held her gaze until the ambulance pulled away, out of the driveway and into the street.

She felt the way she imagined Noah would be coming in for a landing. Her breath caught in her throat, her heart took turns speeding up and slowing down and her stomach felt as if it was flattened against the ceiling. None of it was due to the blaring sirens or how tightly Lacey squeezed her hand. It was love. The eternal kind. The kind that had scared her to death a few days ago, and still did scare her, but also made her glad to be alive.

Meanwhile, the neighbors wandered back home, Julia changed Joey's diaper then buckled him into his car seat and Will and Kristy told Cole to come over if he needed anything. At the airstrip north of Orchard Hill, the Piper Cherokee Noah was piloting touched the ground.

By then Lacey had been admitted and was settled in a bed in a brand-new birthing room in the new wing at the local hospital. Julia arrived with Joey. Marsh Sullivan came next, and although he didn't say it, April believed he'd left the orchards at the onset of the busiest time of the year as much to offer emotional support to his new wife as for Lacey.

April didn't leave Lacey's side. When she wasn't counting contractions, she gave serious thought to her friend's advice.

Despite all the risks and potential for heartache, she'd fallen in love again. She hadn't meant for it to happen, but love wasn't something she'd been able to prevent.

Lacey had insisted April needed to make her move. The more April thought about it the more she knew it was advice she wanted to take.

"Is Noah here yet?" Lacey had been in her hospital room for twenty minutes, and had asked that question too often to count.

"He's in the parking lot," Julia answered, looking at Noah's most recent text.

A nurse bustled into the room. She studied the dials and printouts monitoring the babies' heart rates and Lacey's contractions, and periodically checked the first baby's progress. Lacey's ob-gyn and the pediatrician were en route.

Poor Lacey was in agony. April bathed her face with a cool cloth and she and Julia took turns gripping her hands. Both mothers themselves, they spoke to her only when she was resting during those brief interludes between contractions. They all wagered guesses as to how much the first baby was going to weigh: four and a half pounds, five and Lacey's droll prediction, fifteen.

"Oh, no, not again, not already," she groaned at the onset of yet another contraction.

Just then Noah bounded into the room so like one of the Shackleford horses Cole saw in him. Wearing a hospital gown covering his jeans and shirt, he sidled to his wife's bedside, swept her hair from her face and took her hands.

When the contraction was over, he was decidedly paler than he'd been when he'd arrived. "I never landed a plane so fast from five thousand feet. I was so afraid I would be too late. I'm here now, baby."

The nurse returned with the ob-gyn in tow. It was time for Lacey to push.

Julia and April quietly left the room, giving the couple the privacy such an intimate experience deserved. Marsh took Joey to the cafeteria, and April and Julia found a bench at the end of the hall.

"Who was with you when Joey was born?" April asked, noting the darkening circles beneath Julia's beautiful blue eyes.

"My sixteen-year-old sister, Annie. She runs like the wind and plays the violin like an angel, but she's been a handful ever since she came to live with me. I swear having her there with me was the best birth control lesson she'd ever had."

They shared a smile.

And Julia said, "Marsh said he'd keep Annie if—" Her voice trailed away. Trying again, she said, "I was hoping—" She cast the most loving smile at her husband and son, who were stepping off the elevator at the end of the long corridor.

"What were you hoping?" April asked.

With a deep sigh, Julia said, "I thought, if the worst happens, you and Marsh might—"

"We might what?" April asked. And then, with a dawning realization, she said, "You thought if you die Marsh and I might one day fall in love?"

Julia whispered, "You'd have my blessing. You're wonderful with children. You're kind and quirky and funny and strong. I can't think of anyone I'd feel better about leaving Marsh, Joey and Annie with than you, April."

April knew she had only one chance to say the right thing. How many times had someone told her that Jay was in a better place now, or that the first year was the hardest, or that he was watching over her and the girls, or that it had simply been his time, or that God needed him in heaven? Though well intended, those words always left her feeling hollow inside.

Today, she wanted to insist that Julia wasn't going to die, but that wasn't what her friend needed right now. Cancer was a snide, sniveling enemy. A snake in the grass, it could lay hidden for weeks, months, even years, lulling people into a euphoric sense of hope before randomly rearing up and sinking its deadly fangs deep into flesh and bone.

Placing her hand over Julia's cooler one, she said, "I'm honored, and so very touched. I promise you, if the worst happens, I will do everything I can to help Marsh with Joey, and Annie, too. I'll be a friend to all three of them, the way you've been a friend to me this past year."

"But?" Julia asked.

"I've known Marsh for seven years. He was single for a long time before he met you. After you left Joey on his father's doorstep, Marsh was frantic to find you. He never stopped trusting you or believing you would return the instant you were able. I'm pretty sure he's a one-woman man, Julia. That said, I have to tell you I think you're going to live to be very old."

Julia stared into the distance without smiling. "What about you? Will you take Lacey's advice?"

April considered the question then asked, "What did you do when you came back for Joey?"

Watching her husband swing their beloved toddler onto his shoulders, Julia said, "I had every intention of returning to North Carolina with my son."

"What changed your mind?" April asked.

"Marsh did."

"How?"

Julia's gaze locked with her handsome husband's from twenty feet away. "He opened his arms and I walked into them."

"I don't think it's going to be that easy with Cole."

"Then you're going to have to make sure you make it even more difficult for him to tell you no."

Hmm. April hadn't thought of it that way. What could she do to make it impossible for Cole to walk away? If he loved her, that is.

Her breathing hitched. She'd just discovered the place she needed to begin.

She and Julia went back to Lacey's room with Marsh and Joey. Lacey had been pushing for a long time, but the voices had grown frighteningly faint on the other side of the door. While they waited in the hall, Joey ate a cookie and everyone else held their breath. And then there came the faint mewling cry of a newborn baby.

There were murmurs from inside the room and smiles and tears outside. After a time, they heard the doctor say, "Well, Lacey, are you ready for round two?"

Lacey called her physician a colorful name, and then she called her husband a few as well. Ready or not, it started all over again. By 8:22 p.m., she'd proven three specialists wrong, for Lacey had conceived against all odds, and in a style that was all her own, she'd carried and delivered not one but two small but healthy babies.

When they were finally able to see her, Lacey looked tired and undeniably ethereally beautiful. Though three weeks early, the babies weighed slightly over five pounds and had strong lusty cries. Holding a new daughter in the crook of each arm, Noah was over the moon. The sight of a newborn baby never failed to move April. The sight of two filled her with wonder.

After congratulating his brother and admiring his new nieces, Marsh took his wife and son home to his beloved apple orchards. April held each tiny bundle and marveled at their wispy dark hair, perfect bow lips and tiny fingers and toes.

Looking more serene than April had ever seen her, Lacey said, "Miracles happen, April. Go get yours. Don't do anything I wouldn't do."

"There isn't anything you wouldn't do," April laughed.

"My point exactly."

With a promise to return tomorrow with Gracie and Violet, April rode down in the elevator and walked outside where dusk had turned into darkness. She'd ridden to the hospital in an ambulance, and although there were friends and relatives she could have called to take her home, she decided to walk the eight blocks to her place.

She'd made up her mind what she was going to do. Only time would tell how Cole would take it, and what he would do in return.

It didn't take April long to reach the sidewalk in front of her house. She paused for a moment, for she didn't often take the time to view her home from this perspective.

It was only ten o'clock, but it felt later. A silver quarter moon was rising in the east and a smattering of stars twinkled overhead. It was Saturday night. Someone was having a party down the street, and yet there was a waiting stillness about her house.

There were no outside lights on, and the light from the streetlamps on either corner didn't reach this far. Her gaze was drawn to the soft glow of lamplight coming from inside. Normally, she closed the blinds, but they were wide-open tonight, allowing her a glimpse through her own windows. She could see Julia's amazing watercolor over her sofa. On the dining room table was a vase filled with the dandelions the girls had picked yesterday.

Lights were on upstairs, making the Cape Cod house seem complete in a way it hadn't been until now. It was as if it had been waiting to be finished. It truly was the right time for this project. She prayed it was the right time for her and Cole, too.

Following the sidewalk to the side door, she stopped and sniffed the air. "Cole?"

"I'm out here, April."

She peered into the shadows and saw that he was sitting in the dark at the patio table. "Do I smell cigar smoke?" she asked.

He rose to his feet and she was pretty sure he shook

his head. "Will lit one up before he went home a few minutes ago. He came over under the guise of offering me a cigar leftover after the birth of his last baby, but I'm pretty sure his wife sent him to make sure the girls were all right."

She smiled, for that sounded like Jay's younger brother and his wife. "How were Gracie and Violet?" she asked.

"They were good, although I don't know how you keep up with them. They're asleep on the floor upstairs. It was Grace's idea. I hope it's okay."

"It's more than okay," she said. "Lacey and Noah's babies arrived."

"I heard. Will saw it on Facebook. Everybody's doing okay?"

"There wasn't time for a C-section. And there was no need. She delivered them naturally without any complications. I'm surprised you didn't hear her."

"It was bad?"

"It was good. And noisy. Lacey's not one to hold back. She delivered two healthy, beautiful, perfect baby girls twenty minutes apart. She wasn't supposed to be able to have children. It's a miracle."

He smiled. And she reminded herself to breathe.

"Did her husband make it?"

"She threatened to kill him. Actually, she threatened worse things." At his stare, she said, "Oh, you mean did Noah make it to the hospital in time? Yes. You should see him. He's over the moon."

She sighed. Smiled.

"Oh, I almost forgot. Lacey wanted me to tell you she's naming the twins Colette and Colina. After you."

"What did I do?" he asked, bewildered.

"She's convinced her labor began because she kissed you."

At his horrified expression, she burst into laughter. "She really did tell me to tell you that."

"What are they really naming them?" he asked drolly.

"Olivia Rose after his grandmother and Lenora Renee after hers."

"That's nice," Cole said. "How did you and Jay choose Gracie's and Violet's names?"

"Grace is my middle name. And Jay always brought me violets for my birthday." She smiled at the memory, and found there was mostly joy in it.

With that, she started into the house and he followed.

Immediately the two of them went upstairs. Her daughters lay side by side on pink and yellow sleeping bags spread on the floor of what would soon be a finished bedroom. Both little girls were sound asleep. Cole's power tools had been put away and the floor swept of debris and sawdust. The windows were open, letting in a gentle breeze.

April had checked the progress with the construction of the bedrooms and bathroom every night after Cole left for the day. The partitions were up and all the outside walls were insulated. Yesterday the electrician had finished the rough-in wiring and Cole and a teenager he'd hired had started hanging drywall. On Monday the plumber was scheduled to begin. The rooms were taking shape, but this was the first time she'd seen the purple chalk lines that had been drawn for closets and the bathtub, sink, toilet and shower.

She was intrigued by the other colorful chalk outlines, for it appeared that Gracie and Violet had brought all their sidewalk chalk upstairs. They'd drawn green squares that appeared to be beds complete with pillows, and yellow shapes resembling rectangles for dressers and blue circles for rugs and the usual rainbows, flowers, hearts and butterflies everywhere.

In a deep whisper so close to her ear she warmed ten degrees, Cole said, "They started out in separate rooms. When I checked on them a little while later, Violet had moved over here with Gracie. By then they were both sound asleep and I saw no reason to move them."

April smiled, for her daughters didn't like to be separated. Both of them were wearing their new pajamas. Gracie was covered to her waist with her favorite princess blanket; her stuffed rabbit was tucked under one arm. As usual, Violet had kicked her blanket off.

April bent down to get Violet and Cole scooped Gracie into his strong arms, stuffed rabbit, blanket and all. Her little girls were growing fast. It seemed such a short time ago they were as tiny as Lacey's newborns.

Gracie slept through the ride down to her bed, but Violet opened her eyes as April lowered her to hers. "Hi, Mama," she whispered sleepily.

"Hi, sweet pea."

"Auntie Lacey had her babies."

"I heard," her mother said on a smile.

"The bunnies are getting fat." With that, she snuggled into her pillow and closed her eyes again.

April adjusted blankets and turned on the princess night-light. She and Cole tiptoed from the room.

Perhaps it was the darkness in the hall or the intimacy of sharing something as precious as putting two sleeping little girls to bed. More likely, it was what April had on her mind.

"You're probably exhausted. I should be going," he said, his voice a velvety murmur directly behind her.

"Would you stay for a few minutes?" she asked quietly as she emerged into the dining room.

"Uh. Sure. I guess."

Encouraging, he wasn't.

The light over the table had a dimmer switch and was turned down low. Liking the play of shadows and soft light, she glanced up at Cole. Studying him unhurriedly, she noted the healthy tan of his skin, the dark brown eyes and straight nose, the strong eyebrows and short coffee-colored hair. He had one of those mouths women fantasized about. Just being in the same room with him caused a stirring deep in April's belly.

Lacey probably would have had her shirt off by now, and Chelsea would have given Cole one of her most potent come-hither smiles. Although April would have preferred to be wearing a pretty dress, and it would have been nice if her makeup hadn't all but disappeared, come-hither smiles and striptease acts weren't her style. A glass of wine and candlelight would have created a better atmosphere; she would have settled for running a brush through her hair. But there was no time for any of those things. And really, there was no need. Everything she needed she had within her.

"Is something wrong?" he asked. "Was there a complication with the births or something you haven't mentioned?"

With a shake of her head, she said, "Everyone is fine. Truly, positively radiant, healthy and happy." Her throat bobbled slightly, but she swallowed her nerves and held Cole's gaze. "There's something I need to tell you."

She took a deep breath, and inhaled the scent of pine

boughs and peppermint. It was Cole's unique scent, and it gave her the courage to begin.

"First of all, thank you for staying with the girls. I wasn't expecting that but you helped them, and me, too."

He opened his mouth to speak, but she held up one hand. "You make a wonderful friend." She smiled, and felt heartened when his gaze strayed to her mouth.

He smiled back. He really was doing that more readily now.

He didn't back away when she placed her hand on his arm. Keeping her touch light and her voice soft, she said, "You don't need me to tell you what kind of man you are. I will say this. You're a rarity."

"April, I—"

She placed her fingertips on his lips, for she somehow knew if she didn't finish this now, she never would. "I had the best of intentions. I really did," she said.

His gaze had locked with hers.

Praying this wasn't how Violet had felt when she'd asked for a puppy she couldn't have, April said, "But friendship isn't what I feel for you. It isn't what I want from you."

Okay, he wasn't shaking his head or backing away or calling her crazy, all good things. He wasn't taking her in his arms, either. Hadn't she told Julia he wouldn't make this as easy as Marsh had?

"I want more, Cole."

The air heated, her pulse quickened, and Cole did it all with his steady stare.

He opened his mouth, but no sound came. That was all right. She had more to say anyway. "I want you, Cole."

For five solid wonderful interminable seconds, she

thought he was going to kiss her. His lips parted and a vein pulsed along the side of his tanned neck. A hush fell over the entire house and beyond the windows the night insects started to sing. She probably could have gone up on tiptoe and gotten things rolling, but she was being completely honest, and as such she refused to resort to feminine wiles or seduction tactics.

He swung away from her and started to pace. Like a caged tiger, he went back and forth between the table and the stove before he faced her again.

He was wearing the same jeans he'd worked in today. They fit him like they were made for him, the seams, pockets and fly faded. He was one of those guys who looked good in jeans and a T-shirt, that was all there was to it. The shadow of a beard darkened his jaw, and she'd been right about his hair. It had grown these past two weeks and definitely had wavy tendencies. He was tall, and no matter how many sweets she prepared, she doubted he'd gained an ounce.

"I don't know what to say, April."

Those weren't exactly heady words, but he was being honest, too, so she said, "Say whatever is on your mind."

"I've had a crush on you for a long time," he said, looking for all intents and purposes as if he'd just admitted he was a serial killer.

"A crush?" she asked.

"Feelings," he said.

She wouldn't let herself smile yet. "How long?" she asked.

The sound he made had a lot in common with a man in pain. "Since before Jay died. From the onset, I felt guilty as sin about that. Guiltier than I can say. Don't make this worse."

Oh, she was going to make it worse.

"How could you have had a crush on me? We never met, never spoke until you arrived in Orchard Hill three weeks ago."

"Jay talked about you all the time," he said as if he was feeling miserable. "Some of the guys razzed him, said he was just lonely. Nobody was that perfect. But somehow, I knew better. When he described something about you, I could picture it as if you were standing right there. I imagined it more than I should have, April."

"You had no one waiting for you at home?" she asked softly.

He shook his head.

"You were lonely, Cole. That's all," she said. "There's certainly nothing wrong with that." She could tell he wasn't appeased. "I love Jay," she said. As confusion settled behind his eyes, she said, "I'll always love him. I think you know that. But I love you, too. In fact, I'm *in* love with you."

He started toward her, and she held her breath in anticipation of being swept into his embrace. But he stopped short of touching her and held perfectly still as if poised on the edge of a high ledge. Without a word, he backed away, turned on his heel and left.

Just left. As in, he walked right out the door without looking back.

She couldn't believe he did that.

The screen had barely bounced closed and she had barely begun to make sense of his reaction to her honest declaration when the door opened again and he bounded back in. "This is a fine mess," he said on a growl.

A caged tiger, definitely.

"I promised Jay I wouldn't do this."

His large hands cupped her shoulders. And he kissed her.

It was a hard kiss, a searing kiss, an I-would-die-without-this-kiss kiss. Her eyes fluttered closed, and a song filled her chest, for it was a genuine kiss, a heartfelt kiss.

She'd dreamed of this kiss.

Tilting her head a little, she wound her arms around his neck and opened her mouth beneath his. The first time she'd kissed him had lit a candle in the darkness inside her; in a way it had brought her back to life. This was different. This was primal, and made her feel as if she'd somehow gone back to the beginning only to discover she'd been here before. Which made no sense.

She didn't have to make sense of Cole's kiss. He could go on kissing her forever, and it would make sense enough.

His kiss was turbulent, his mouth hard and hot, his body harder and hotter. He held her to him, his mouth moving across hers, his hands gliding down her back, molding her closer.

She wanted this, reveled in this, but she wanted so much more. She wanted to take this to another level. To claim him physically, emotionally, as her own, and to be claimed by him the same way.

It had been so long since she'd experienced this euphoria, this heady need, this melting and this sense of belonging. She moaned.

And it stopped him like a slap. When he lifted his head and opened his eyes, eased backward and finally removed his hands, she could see he wasn't happy about any of it.

"You don't have to stop, Cole."

"I do. I—Jay—"

"We both know Jay isn't here," she said quietly. She was pretty sure his derisive snort wasn't directed at her. "Did Jay know?" she heard herself ask. At his somewhat bewildered expression, she added, "Did he know how you felt? About your crush, I mean?"

She wanted to understand Cole's haunted expression.

"No," he said.

"Then when did you promise him?"

"At the cemetery shortly after I arrived in Orchard Hill," he said. "I told him why I was here and I assured him it had nothing to do with the way his descriptions of his life here in Orchard Hill had somehow turned into fantasies that infiltrated my dreams. I promised Jay I would finish the upstairs for you and the girls and that I would watch over you while I was here, but I wouldn't try to walk in his shoes or try to fill them. And then I slept soundly for the first time in months. I just broke my promise to him. I'm not the kind of man you deserve, April. I can't be that man. I'm s—"

"Don't you dare say you're sorry," she sputtered. "Of course you can."

He shook his head. It seemed he had nothing left to say then.

"You do realize you can't make promises to people who have died."

He held perfectly still when she knew he wanted to argue.

"Is the real me less desirable than the figment of your imagination? Is that it?"

"Of course that's not it."

She stood in silence waiting for him to explain his

denial. Then it occurred to her. "You aren't going to let yourself return my love because of Jay."

"This has nothing to do with love."

"What else is there?" she asked.

He started to pace again. Watching him, she barely moved.

He finally swung around and faced her again. "I think Jay brought me here, but not to take his place."

Looking at him, she knew it would do no good to tell him that no one could take another's place. There was a battle raging within Cole. It made no sense to her. But if he wouldn't let himself love her, there was nothing she could do about it.

"I know you don't want to hear it," he said. "But I am sorry. You deserve better. You deserve happiness. I'm just not in a position to give it to you."

She didn't know how long she stared at him. Finally, heaving a sigh, she said, "All right then. You might as well go."

"I don't want to leave it like this. The last thing I want to do is hurt you. I don't want things to be awkward between us."

"I can't guarantee anything right now," she said.

She needed to think. She needed to decide where she'd gone wrong.

"April."

"I'll see you on Monday, Cole."

Duly dismissed, he left, albeit reluctantly. And she knew he wouldn't return before Monday, wouldn't walk back through that door within seconds of leaving as he had on two previous occasions. She knew he wouldn't take her in his arms and tell her he loved her. Even though she was almost certain now that he did.

He said he'd promised Jay. She didn't believe for a moment that was all there was to it. There was more. Something he wasn't telling her.

Surprise, surprise.

She bolted the door and turned out the light without waiting for his headlights to disappear. She'd just offered Cole her heart and he'd handed it back to her. As far as she was concerned, she was entitled to a flare of temper.

She didn't know whether to bang her head against the wall, stomp her feet or cry. No, crying was out of the question. She'd cried enough this past year. She didn't stomp her feet or bang her head against the wall, either, for she'd outgrown temper tantrums a long time ago.

Doing the next best thing, she ran a warm bath, added bubbles and sank into the soft, soothing water. After the bubbles had dissipated and the water had cooled, she pulled the plug, dried off and donned pajamas. Wearing Jay's robe, she wandered through her quiet house. Outside, crickets chirruped and the late night breeze wafting through the screen rattled the blinds she'd closed.

She checked the girls and studied every framed photograph in the living room. She stared for a long time at those of Jay. She missed that smile, the way his eyes crinkled and the way she'd been so sure their love would last.

She missed his presence, his strength, the honor that had always filled him. She missed everything about him, even the way he left his shoes all over the house and the way he squeezed the toothpaste tube from the top.

She missed Cole, too. It was true. Already, she missed him. And he wasn't in some far-off realm few living humans had ever glimpsed. He was right here in Orchard Hill. She sighed, for he might as well have been on another planet.

No one ever said love was easy. The thought came, unbidden, almost as if someone had whispered it in her ear.

With a sigh, she slipped out of Jay's robe and hung it on the hook on the back of her bedroom door where Jay had left it. She ran her hand down the lapels, but didn't bury her face in the soft fabric, for she knew Jay's scent was completely gone now.

By the time she finally crawled into bed, she'd gone over and over everything she and Cole had said to one another tonight. She knew what she had to do.

It was time.

Chapter Nine

Cole was dreaming.

He hadn't expected to sleep, much less dream. But he was dreaming. April was here in his room at the Stone Inn. They were in his bed, her hands were on his chest, her legs tangling with his.

Her wavy brown hair caressed his chest, a silky curtain on either side of her face. Her breasts were pebbled, her lips swollen from his kiss. Their clothes lay scattered about his floor, but there was nothing scattered about her intentions. Or his. He'd learned her by heart, and he was going to have her. With a seductive smile, she was determined to know him just as intimately.

Even in his sleep, he knew he was dreaming. He knew because the clothing he'd shed wasn't civilian wear.

He felt himself sinking deeper into the oblivion of sleep. With it everything began to change. He struggled against it, because he didn't want to leave his bed, didn't want to leave his dream of April.

But suddenly he heard the discordant din of gunfire. The sound came again, closer now. Jay was with him. They were on the battlefield, together again, their movements synchronized, their thoughts one. All around them was the grit of sand and the searing relentless heat of the unforgiving desert.

Men yelled and orders were shouted. According to intel, the opposition was keeping children in a building they were using as their headquarters some one hundred yards away. It was to be a carefully orchestrated rescue, but something was wrong. He and Jay were crawling through thick black smoke, facing an enemy they could sense but couldn't see.

No matter where they turned, their foes closed in on them from all sides. They couldn't give up. They couldn't give in.

They had lives to save.

All at once they rose above the deafening roar of bombs exploding and the gagging stench of war. Flying now, they could see their comrades down below where the war raged on.

But the war raged in the sky, too, for their worst nightmare had followed them. With a reprehensible depraved hunger to inflict unspeakable suffering, the beast drew closer, its intent as foul-smelling as its breath. They tried to outdistance it, to outmaneuver it, but it persisted. Their weapons useless, they had to rely on cunning and stamina and speed.

They were winded, nearly worn-out, but they couldn't panic, couldn't falter. They couldn't give up. They had lives to save.

They escaped their pursuers, hiding for a moment behind the rubble of an old building. Suddenly, the area swarmed with people, a hundred, two hundred, more.

He and Jay became separated among the throngs. Desperate but unquestionably determined to find his war-brother, Cole methodically searched every face.

And then he saw him. Jay lay on the white sand, the front of his uniform red with blood. Cole clawed his way through the throngs to Jay's side. Jay opened his eyes, looked into Cole's, and whispered, "I'm counting on you."

Before his eyes Jay faded like vapor on thin air.

Cole jolted awake. Sat up. Then held perfectly still. With his heart thundering in his chest, he tried to get his bearings.

The lamp was still on next to his bed, as was the TV across the room. He'd fallen asleep wearing his jeans.

He aimed the remote at the TV and pulled the chain on the antique lamp. Now that it was dark and quiet, he got out of bed and padded barefoot to the window. Drawing the curtain aside, he looked down upon the meandering river where reflections of a quarter moon danced on its rippling surface.

There was no war but for the one raging within him. It was a long time before his heart beat a normal rhythm.

He understood the first portion of his dream, for before he'd fallen asleep he'd stretched out on the bed with April's kisses still fresh on his lips, her lush curves imprinted along the entire length of him. His body knew what it wanted. His heart wanted the same thing. Except for Jay's final words, the second dream was identical to the dreams he'd had before Jay was killed. "I'm counting on you," Jay had uttered in tonight's dream.

A soldier relied on gut instinct, and Cole's instincts screamed that his presence in Orchard Hill hadn't been happenstance.

He knew that dreams were often wrought with images that could be interpreted many different ways, and misinterpreted, as well. There had been times in his life when aspects of his dreams had happened before his eyes. It had frightened him as a child, but he'd learned to pay attention to them.

Through his window, he saw a light in the sky, and followed a jet with his gaze until he lost it in the stars.

There was a part of Cole that would always be a soldier, maybe always had been. Perhaps that was why he'd been a loner much of his life.

He didn't bank on dreams or on superstition. They were unreliable. A soldier relied on gut instinct.

Right now, his gut was on fire.

Anyone who didn't know what gut instinct was had never been to war. His gut instinct had saved his comrades' lives more than once. And his comrades had saved his. He didn't need proof beyond that.

For nearly fifteen months, Cole had lived with the knowledge that Jay had died instead of him. Cole had dreamed of death before the ambush, but Jay had opted to follow his own instincts. Cole and Jay had been equals in every sense of the word. They thought alike, kept their wits about them at all times and believed that goodness would prevail—even though too often it seemed hopeless.

When the attack came, Jay was covering Cole, but seeing his best friend in the sights of the enemy, he'd charged ahead, rapidly firing his weapon. Others took up the battle. Intel had been right about the innocent children who were hostages. Because of Jay's heroism, none of them had been harmed.

If not for Jay, Cole would have been the one who'd died that day. And all the people back home who'd loved Jay would have been spared their grief. Violet and Gracie would still have their father, April would still have her husband, and Jim and JoAnn Avery would still have their son.

Cole didn't know why it hadn't gone the other way. If it had, he wouldn't have been half as missed.

Now, after fifteen months, Cole was dreaming again. April loved him. He hadn't seen that coming, and yet his longing for her was so acute he would have given his life for one night like the one he'd dreamed he and April had.

Every instinct told him to resist. No matter what he wanted. What he needed. Until he understood why, he had to remain focused on the vow he'd made to himself and the promise he'd given his best friend.

April loved him.

Cole released all the breath he'd been holding. Drawing another, he knew resisting her was going to test every instinct he had.

April folded the last of Jay's freshly laundered dress shirts and started sorting his ties. She pictured him tying his tie, and slipping it off. He'd had one of those physiques that looked good no matter what he wore. She closed her eyes, for she'd tried to do this without thinking, without remembering, but couldn't.

Last summer a kindhearted eighty-two-year-old widow who'd lost her husband of sixty years had told

April she would know when it was time to take this step. It was time. But it wasn't easy.

She placed his suits loosely in an oblong box on her bed. Closing the lid, she began filling another with the shirts she'd folded, and then his ties.

Even after she'd made the decision to do this, she'd put it off another day. She'd finally begun this arduous undertaking yesterday afternoon. She hadn't gotten far when the girls had begged to go to the park. She'd prepared a picnic lunch and had taken them to the playground and then to the hospital to see Noah and Lacey's babies. The remainder of the task of going through Jay's things had been left for today.

Now, on this pretty summer Tuesday, she was finishing what she'd started. She put all Jay's sports T-shirts, college sweatshirts and jerseys in a box and stored it on the top shelf of her closet in the event Violet and Gracie or one of Jay's brothers or sisters wanted them one day.

Next, she opened his top dresser drawer. Her fingers trembled as she brought out his wallet. Like she had so many times already, she brought one of his possessions to her nose and sniffed. The wallet smelled of fine leather; like everything else, it carried no lingering scent of Jay.

She opened the tri-fold, and leafed through photos of her and the girls. His driver's license was still where he'd left it, as was the fifty-dollar bill he'd kept hidden in a secret sleeve.

Spotting a piece of paper in the same compartment, she withdrew the small square and carefully unfolded it. Her fingers went to her trembling lips as she read the note she'd tucked into Jay's pocket before he left for work on their first wedding anniversary. She'd had no idea he'd saved this. Reading it again, she flung herself across her bed and cried the way she had the day she'd burned their mattress.

When she was spent, she dried her face, refolded the note and lovingly tucked it back into the wallet for safekeeping, then placed the wallet in a small box along with a sprig of lavender. She added the cuff links she'd given him the last Christmas they'd celebrated together, his dog tags and Purple Heart, and a smattering of other mementos she couldn't bear to part with.

His casual wear was going to a local church group preparing for a missionary trip to the Appalachians. She was donating his dress clothes to a local nonprofit agency that helped the homeless and those living in halfway houses prepare for job interviews.

Now Jay's portion of the closet and his dresser drawers were empty. She wondered if she would ever be able to use them. She felt empty, too, as if she was depleted of something vital. Reminding herself that doing this hadn't made Jay's death any more real or him any more gone, she changed her clothes and finger combed her hair then started for the door, only to stop, her feet rooted to the floor. For a moment, she actually considered putting all his things back where they'd been. But what good would it do? It wouldn't bring him back. Nothing could do that.

Hoping she didn't look as ravaged as she felt, she poked her head into the living room where Gracie and Violet were watching the last portion of their favorite animated movie. Finding them content and occupied, she carried the first box to her SUV. Careful to step around the small puddle left over from last night's rain, she made trip after trip from her house to her vehicle.

Each time she returned to her bedroom for another armful, she looked at Jay's robe hanging on the hook on the back of the door. She'd purposefully left it behind, and seeing it, touching it, just knowing it was there made her feel better somehow. It belonged here, a part of him, and here was where it would stay.

She had room in her car for only one more cardboard carton when she finally crossed paths with Cole. He'd arrived for work this morning at a few minutes after eight as he always did. They'd exchanged good mornings, and he'd drunk half a cup of coffee while Violet and Gracie told him all about the dog they'd played with in the park yesterday.

"Guess what his name was?" Grace had asked.

"Horse!" Violet retorted before Cole had a chance to guess. "He weighs more than both of us together!"

He'd been smiling when he glanced at April. She was the first to look away.

She wasn't angry. Not anymore. She was sad. And she was so tired of feeling this way.

"What do you have there?" he asked her now from the middle of the sidewalk.

Rather than commenting on how tired he looked, she said, "Some things I'm donating."

Again, she was the first to look away.

"Let me get that for you." Leaving her no choice, he took the cumbersome box right out of her hands.

Eyeing all the others already stacked in the back of her SUV, he said, "You're parting with Jay's things?"

If only there hadn't been such reverence in his deep voice. She sighed, and in lieu of an answer, she reclaimed the box and fit it into the last open slot. She pushed a button and they both stepped back as the hatch on her vehicle closed.

He looked at her, stared actually. Twice, he started to say something. Twice, he stopped.

Well, then. As they said in old movies, it was time to get this show on the road.

Bristling a little for no good reason, she said, "There's a pitcher of fresh lemonade in the refrigerator. I bought more ginger ale as well. As soon as the girls' movie is over, we'll be on our way. If you get thirsty while we're gone, help yourself to a cold beverage."

She could feel his eyes on her as she started back toward the house, but he made no comment. Really, she thought, after Saturday night, what was left for him to say?

He'd admitted he had feelings for her, and had for a long time. But something was holding him back, and he was the only one who could break through the barrier he'd imposed.

And if he never does?

Closing her eyes, she sighed again. She'd grown weary of wretched thoughts like that one.

The girls were at the door suddenly. Yelling loud enough for everyone in the neighborhood to hear, they informed April that their movie was over. She hurried inside to get them ready to help her donate items their father didn't need in heaven.

She'd known this emotional day would come.

It was time.

Walking out April's door Saturday night had been the hardest thing Cole had ever done, more difficult even than starting a business from scratch or fighting a war. In those instances, he'd known his next move.

He'd told her he didn't want things to be awkward between them. What was between them was awkward as hell.

They spent a good share of their day in the same house, but no matter how close they came physically, whether it was in a doorway or on the stairs or even outside, there was a chasm between them.

He couldn't very well tell her he'd taken a giant step backward emotionally because his gut churned every time he came close to her. He needed to focus. It was like his old high school football coach had told him and his teammates after the last practice before every game. No dating, no sex the night before. They needed to keep a clear head. Every man knew sex was the ultimate distraction.

What a way to go. But this wasn't some game. Until he figured out what the hell held him back, he needed to give April a wide berth.

He didn't trust himself to tell her the reason. More accurately he didn't trust her to accept his reason. She was a woman in love. God knew that was as distracting as the lure of sex.

She wasn't happy about his new reserve.

She wasn't impolite. But the camaraderie of the previous weeks was gone. She hadn't asked him about any more of his animal associations. She no longer pressed him to tell her how he saw her. But she'd baked something again today, and she still smiled, although rarely at him; she still did the myriad things single mothers did. Earlier he'd heard her reading to Violet and Gracie in her soft lilting voice, and heard her encouraging them to read, to count and to pretend. She was preparing them for school while she got ready to return to her teaching career.

She'd boxed up Jay's things. She was moving on with her life.

With or without Cole.

The girls seemed oblivious to the undercurrents that stretched like taut wires between their mother and their father's best friend. Thank God for that, at least. They deserved a happy childhood. All children did.

Violet and Gracie were so open, so innocent and bright. One blonde, the other brown-haired, both were the perfect combinations of Jay and April.

They'd been wide-eyed with wonder yesterday when he'd told them that baby rabbits were called kittens, or kits, just like baby cats. While he'd had their attention he'd explained that kits generally left their nest when they were two weeks old. The rabbits Gracie and Violet had discovered had to be nearing that age.

The girls had looked at one another as they silently communicated in what April had once called "twinspeak." And he'd known they understood that one day soon they would check on the rabbits and find the nest beneath the Daddy Tree deserted.

Cole missed talking to April, missed her quirky questions and amazing insights. This wasn't easy for him. Hell, it was excruciating, for he yearned to drag her into his arms. He held back. He didn't know why. Whatever it was, it scared the hell out of him.

He was standing at his tailgate, attempting to change the carbide blade on his saw when April and the girls came out of the house again. Gracie and Violet wore shorts and sandals and sunglasses. Gracie carried a glittery purse and Violet wore a feather boa. Each girl's hair was wound into a delicate-looking braid that encircled her head like a crown.

April's hair waved long and loose halfway down her back, the sides pulled away from her face and secured with turquoise clasps. She wore a filmy lavender shirt and yellow shorts. He remembered when she'd asked him about his favorite color. He'd told her he didn't have one. If she'd asked him today, he would have said it was whatever color she was wearing.

She didn't ask him, though. And she wouldn't. Not anymore. He missed that, too.

"Someone's here, Mama," Gracie said.

Everyone, including Cole, glanced at the man walking up the driveway. Violet hopped out of the car and stood beside her sister, who'd been, in her mother's words, lollygagging.

"May I help you?" April asked, her tone friendly.

Since it would have been impolite to stare, Cole sized the man up quickly then returned to his task at the tailgate of his truck. Clean-cut, the man looked to be in his late thirties. Of medium build, he had sandy blond hair, and wore baggy chinos and a buttoned shirt. Just your average Joe.

He stopped several feet from April. "I'm Nathan Hampton. I've only recently joined Jake Nichols's veterinarian practice. If I'm keeping you from an appointment, I can come back later."

Cole fit the wrench over the nut holding the old blade in place and added *polite* and *conscientious* to his impressions of the man. Normally, he would have noticed similarities to some animal by now. Maybe he was losing the ability.

He feared that what he was losing was April.

"You're not keeping us from an appointment," she was saying. "Is there something I can do for you, Mr. Hampton?"

"Nathan," he said.

The smile Nathan gave April left a bad taste in Cole's mouth.

"My dog and I moved into the house down on the corner last week," he said.

"You have a dog?" Violet was quick to ask.

Nathan Hampton was smiling as he answered. "I do. Her name is Roxie. She's the reason I'm here." He turned to April. "She was a rescue. A case of terrible neglect, but you'd never know it today. She's the sweetest dog I've ever had." He held his hand a few feet above the ground. "Roughly three years old, she's about this tall and weighs thirty pounds. The only time her tail stops wagging is when she's asleep or afraid."

"What's she afraid of?" Gracie asked, obviously intrigued.

"Loud noises, mostly." He glanced at April. Up, down and up again.

Cole gripped the wrench with his right hand. It kept him from grabbing Nathan Hampton by the scruff of the neck and throwing him off April's property, a bit of an overreaction, not to mention against the law.

"How old are your little girls?" Nathan asked.

"They'll be five next Thursday," April said proudly.

Cole remembered when she'd mentioned their upcoming birthday, but he hadn't known the twins would turn five so soon. The bolt he was reefing on finally loosened with a loud clank nobody seemed to notice but him. Feeling surlier by the second, he removed the old blade and reached for the new one.

"Is that your husband?" Good old Nathan had lowered his voice.

With a shake of her head, April replied, "He's a carpenter and a friend of my late husband's."

A friend of Jay's. Not a friend of hers. Cole deserved that.

Etiquette dictated that he acknowledge the other man. He did so quickly, and noticed that the veterinarian's ears seemed to have perked up considerably now that he knew April was single.

"Is your loss recent?" he asked.

"A little over a year ago."

"That's too bad," he said.

Nathan's interest intensified. If Cole recognized it from twenty feet away, she had to see it, too.

"You were saying something about your dog?" she prompted.

"Oh." He shot her a hundred-watt smile. "Yes, as I was saying, animals, dogs in particular, never forget their past. She's sometimes skittish and she's terrified of sudden loud noises. She woke me up last night around two. Even though my backyard is fenced, I always go out with her. We were on our way back in when the storm let loose. She bolted when she heard the thunder. I don't know how she fit between the boards in the fence. I called and called but she was gone."

"She still hasn't come home?" April asked.

Nathan shook his head, and Cole had to admit his worry seemed genuine.

"I walked the neighborhood all night looking for her," Nathan Hampton said. "I've taken her on long walks every day since we moved in. I'm hoping she finds her way back home." He reached into his back pocket and brought out his phone. "Here's a picture of her. Have you seen her?"

Okay. The guy had good reason to sidle closer to April. That didn't mean Cole had to like it. He finished tightening the nut over the new saw blade and tried not to bite through his cheek.

"She's an adorable dog, but I'm afraid I haven't seen her," April said.

He showed the photo to Gracie and Violet next. Their eyes round, they pressed themselves to April's side, winding their arms around her legs.

"I'm getting a puppy for my birthday," Violet declared.

"What my daughter meant to say," April intoned, "is she asked for a puppy for her birthday."

Nathan Hampton smiled all around and said, "I'd be happy to help with that. Meanwhile, if you see a spotted brown-and-yellow dog, would you let me know?"

"Of course," April said.

He patted his chest pocket. Bringing out an embossed business card, he looked around for something to write with. Spying Cole's carpenter's pencil, he jogged over and said, "Mind if I borrow this, buddy?"

Without waiting for a reply that Cole would have been hard-pressed to make, he grabbed the pencil and jotted something on the back of the small card. Offering it to April, he said, "The clinic's phone number is on the front. My cell number is on the back. You can call me day or night."

Again with that hundred-watt smile.

"Maybe after I find Roxie, you and your daughters

would like to come down and meet her. She's amazing with children."

April might have replied, but Cole couldn't hear for the roaring in his ears. The veterinarian turned easily and jogged back the way he'd come, tossing Cole the pencil on his way by.

Cole saw red. And then he saw green, the color of jealousy.

Needing to move, he threw the old blade in the trash bin on his way toward the house. Violet and Gracie scrambled up into their seats in the SUV. "Bye, Cole!" they called in unison.

He smiled for their sakes.

April was helping Gracie buckle her seat belt, her back to him. She was a good mother, and a beautiful woman. A hair shy of five-five, she had an amazing body, gorgeous hair and gold-flecked eyes that were going to be impossible to forget.

The smile she'd given the good veterinarian had been easy, unencumbered and held nothing back. She hadn't smiled at Cole that way since Saturday night.

It had been three days since he'd inhaled the flowery scent of her shampoo, since he'd felt her hands come to rest on his shoulders, her breath warm on his neck, since he'd held her soft curves against the hard length of his body and covered her mouth with his. Those three days felt like a lifetime ago.

Once the girls were buckled in, April got behind the wheel. She backed carefully out of her driveway. The twins waved to him, but as far as Cole could tell, April didn't look at him again.

He didn't blame her. What woman as beautiful, responsive and as kind as she was could put on a false front after telling a man she loved him and having him say thanks but no thanks?

No one with her heart, her soul. Or her attitude.

A part of Cole had fallen in love with her while listening to Jay's colorful and oftentimes humorous stories of their life here in Orchard Hill. Now that he knew April personally, he realized those feelings had been but the tip of the iceberg. What he felt now was all-encompassing and so strong it had become a physical ache.

She seemed to be nearing the final phase of her grief.

She was ready to move on. And he didn't know how he would bear to stand by and watch her fall in love with somebody else.

Cole had made a silent promise to Jay when he'd stood at his grave. He'd kept that promise. He hadn't tried to take Jay's place. April hadn't asked him to. She wanted something different from him. Something more.

And yet he held back. What was wrong with him? Did he have a defect? A fatal flaw? Or was it something else? Cole had better figure it out before it was too late.

Chapter Ten

April wasn't herself.

For days she'd been wandering aimlessly through her house, vacillating between moping and snarling. Right now she was leaning toward snarling. Maybe she should shatter some plates against the wall. Or perhaps she should cut her hair. With kitchen scissors.

But she liked her dinnerware. And her hair.

She knew what the problem was. It rhymed with *pole*. As in she shouldn't want to touch him with a ten-foot pole.

But she did want to touch Cole. She wanted to kiss him thoroughly. She also wanted to throttle him.

She wasn't a violent person. It wasn't as if she never got angry. Dragging her mattress outside and setting a match to it had pretty much proven that. But this was different. Cole hadn't died. He was right here. In this very house.

So close but so far away. She rolled her eyes at herself

because now she was citing song lyrics. She couldn't even mope with original style.

Cole had been up and down the stairs and back and forth through the kitchen a hundred times these past several days. He'd coordinated subcontractors, nailed and cut and trimmed and painted. The upstairs was almost finished. The hardwood floor was down and the doors were on their hinges. Matching chandeliers fit for two young princesses were hanging from the freshly painted ceilings.

On Monday the bathroom tile installers were coming back to grout. The bathtub, shower, vanity and commode were all already installed. The bathroom needed faucets and mirrors and towel bars and the bedrooms closet rods and doors and a few other odds and ends. It wouldn't be long before the project would be finished.

Cole would return to Rochester. And she would have no choice but to let him.

They were running out of time for him to work through his issue. She wasn't asking for explanations. Anyone who'd loved and lost as she had understood that things happened to people, life happened to people, and it created wounds that cut deep. Not everything needed to be dissected, placed under a microscope and then shared. Sometimes the only way to live peacefully was to release the pain, to hold it in your hand and let it float away. If Cole loved her, all she wanted, all she needed, was for him to call her name and open his arms to her. That wasn't asking for much, and yet it was everything.

"April?"

"Yes?" Was that really her voice, so breathless and hopeful? So pathetic.

Cole was at the door. She was outside. She forgot why.

Her hair blew across her cheek. It wasn't until she raised her hand to brush the strands away that she remembered she was holding the mail. Transferring the bills and junk mail to her other hand, she tucked her hair behind one ear and looked closely at Cole.

He stood leaning against the doorframe, one hand holding the screen door open. There was pink paint on his pant leg, and purple on his forearm. Even paint-spattered, he had a heroic air about him.

It occurred to her that neither of them was saying anything. Since he was the one who'd called her name, the floor was all his.

"I didn't see the girls inside," he said. "Are they out here?"

She shook her head.

"The paint is dry. I wanted to show them their rooms."

"They're not here," she said. "They're spending the night with their grandparents."

"So you have the night to yourself?" he asked.

She nodded. Giving a little, she smiled, too. *Ask me out. Ask me to stay here with you. We'll order in. We'll talk. Or we won't talk. We'll make love. We'll make memories. We'll begin the rest of our lives.* Mentally she beamed those thoughts to him with all her might.

He drew himself up to his full height and said, "That's nice of them. It'll do you good to have a night off. Have you decided what you're going to do?"

Obviously it was impossible to beam thoughts through that thick skull.

"Yes," she said.

She gave him to the count of five, which should have

been plenty of time for him to invite her out or to invite himself in. Five long seconds. And nothing.

"I'm going out," she said. It was possible she'd sounded slightly petulant, but so be it.

She didn't tell him to step aside. She didn't say he was in her way. She didn't hit him with anything, not even a ten-foot pole. She set her jaw, charged up the steps and ducked under the elbow with the purple paint on it. She kept going, kept putting one foot in front of the other even as she closed her eyes, because the scent of peppermint and pine boughs and crisp thin winter air came with her.

She put the mail on the kitchen table and put away the plate, fork and glass Cole had used and washed. It was a little after four. Jim and JoAnn had been keeping the girls one evening every month since Jay died. It made Jay's parents happy, and it was healthy for Grace and Violet to be away from her once in a while.

At first she'd hated it, and stayed home and cried. When that got old, she'd visited friends. Sometimes they took in a movie or stayed in and talked. Tonight was going to be different.

She'd said she was going out. And April Avery never lied. It seemed she had a phone call to make and an evening to plan.

Cole was pacing.

It was only eight o'clock and already the night seemed endless.

After folding up the drop cloths and taking care of his tools, he'd been ready to leave April's at six, the time he always finished for the day. Normally she was in the kitchen preparing dinner with the girls then.

Today the kitchen had been deserted.

Hearing the click of heels in the hallway, he'd called, "I'm going, April. Do you want me to come back tomorrow or would you prefer I wait until—"

His voice trailed away along with his train of thought, for April had entered the kitchen. *Whoa. Wow.*

She'd worn casual skirts and crisp pants and even short shorts. This was the first time he'd seen her in a dress like this one. The color of honey, it flowed over her like liquid gold. The shoulders were cut away, showcasing her strong, slender arms and the delicate edges of her collarbones. Cut just low enough in the front to allow a glimpse of the top swells of her breasts, the dress hugged her waist and flared out a little over her hips, stopping just above her knees.

"Does this look okay?" she'd asked.

"Yes." He'd swallowed. "You look nice. Amazing, actually."

"Are you sure? Because this is the fourth thing I've tried on. I haven't been shopping in ages and everything I own is ugly or out of style or both."

"I'm sure."

Ugly? Out of style? Was she kidding? The color of her dress brought out the gold flecks in her eyes, which looked luminous surrounded by her thick black lashes. And the way the dress fit her—the only way she could have possibly looked better was if she slipped out of it.

Her skin was flawless, most likely further enhanced by makeup, although she had a light touch. Her lips were shiny and the color of a ripe peach.

His mouth had watered. His body had heated. He needed to get out of there.

She did that thing women did with their hair, flipping it over her shoulder without touching it, sending it cascading down her back in a riot of soft five-shades-of-beautiful curls.

"Tomorrow morning's fine," she'd said. At his blank expression, she continued, "Isn't that what you asked? If you should come back tomorrow morning or Monday? Whatever you want to do, whatever you think is best is fine with me."

What he wanted to do and what he did were polar opposites. She'd started talking about shoes and changing into something else, and he'd left before he offered to lend a hand.

He'd driven to the inn. And paced. He'd showered. And paced. He'd put on clean clothes and wandered down to the desk for a ghost update from Harriet Ferris. He now walked down to the river and pitched a few dozen stones in, then wandered back up to his room and ordered a pizza. He turned on the TV. Turned it off again.

And paced some more.

The sun was heading down; it was almost nine. It set an hour later here in Michigan than it did in upstate New York. He wondered what April was doing, who she was doing it with and if she was still wearing that dress.

The new veterinarian had stopped over earlier today. He'd been passing out Lost Dog fliers, and gave one to April. He'd probably asked her to have dinner with him.

Or something.

Normally Cole had a steel stomach, so the pizza wasn't to blame for the sick feeling in the pit of his stomach. He tried not to imagine anybody helping her out of her dress. Anybody except him.

He looked around his comfortably furnished room

and recalled Harriet's latest ghost story. He wasn't afraid of the ghost, if there really was one. But the thought of waiting out the endless night imagining April with some other man was enough to have him reaching for his phone and his keys.

April hadn't been to Bell's Tavern since it had re-opened. Actually, she'd only ever been inside during the day, for until Ruby O'Toole, Ruby Sullivan now, had bought it last year, Lacey had lived in the small apartment above it. When Lacey's father had owned the tavern it had been the seediest place in town.

Other than going to a favored sports bar over by the college once in a while, Jay and April hadn't been into the bar scene. She preferred dinner and plays or cards with friends. Bell's Tavern now had a fabulous reputation. There was live music on the weekends and dancing, billiard tournaments every Thursday and card playing in the back every day of the week. It featured locally brewed beer and drinks with names such as Dynamite, Howl at the Moon, Fountain of Youth and Kerfuffle.

April's Kerfuffle sat in front of her. Chelsea was drinking wine.

April was sitting with a few close friends in a local tavern in downtown Orchard Hill, and yet she felt as if she were on another planet. She'd been out alone since Jay had died, but tonight was the first time she'd gone out as a single woman.

Cole hadn't been able to take his eyes off her when she'd first put on this dress. At least she knew she looked okay.

The band tonight was a local country western group;

the music was lively, the drinks were flowing and the atmosphere was jovial. It was ten o'clock, too early for her to go home.

"Don't look, April," Chelsea said, "but there's a certain guy you know over there who has a radar lock on you. News alert. He's coming this way."

April's hopes soared. She glanced up as casually as possible. "Oh," she said, praying her disappointment wasn't obvious. "Hello, Nathan."

The veterinarian smiled. He really had a nice smile. "Mind if I sit down?" he asked.

The only empty chair at the table was adjacent to hers. He took it. April introduced him to her friends. They were all saying hello when Tiffany, their harried waitress, appeared.

As Nathan ordered a beer on tap, Bernadette Fletcher, April's tall, unassuming neighbor nudged April and said, "Isn't that Cole Cavanaugh?"

Cole was taking an empty stool at the bar. Even in faded jeans and a white collared shirt, the cuffs rolled up, he had a soldier's air about him. Chelsea, who was wearing a little black dress and looking as pretty as always, was on her way back from the restroom. She stopped at the bar and spoke to him. He glanced over— and caught April looking. Of course he caught her. The way her luck was running she would probably spill her drink and lose a contact, too. She groaned inwardly, but since Cole already knew she was watching, she saw no reason to stop.

He shook his head at whatever Chelsea said. She appeared to be doing a little cajoling, a natural ability of hers. Again he shook his head. With a shrug, Chelsea continued back to their table, and a pretty brunette took the stool next to Cole's. April dragged her gaze back to her friends.

The new owner, Ruby Sullivan made the rounds. A tall, quirky redhead, Ruby asked if they'd seen the picture of the local ghost. She was referring to a picture Harriet Ferris had taken at the inn; it had gone viral. Everyone was talking about it.

Tiffany returned with Nathan's beer. "Have you seen the picture of the ghost?" she asked as well. "I was in a wedding last weekend. The entire wedding party stayed at the inn." From her pocket Tiffany pulled a copy of the photo that had been all over the local social media circuit. "See this? Clearly, that's a ghost."

April supposed the image looked a little like a ghost. Maybe. Kind of.

"Wait a minute," Chelsea declared. "Are you saying you saw her?"

"Saw her, heard her, felt her. And her dog."

"You're certain it's a woman?"

"A dog, you said?" the new veterinarian cut in.

"She's definitely a woman," Tiffany told Chelsea.

"Tell me the ghost dog isn't a medium-sized spotted dog," Nathan insisted. "Mine's missing."

"It's not. It looks like a German shepherd."

"I heard it's a wolf," someone else said.

Speculation regarding the ghost woman and her wolf-dog continued. April's mind wandered, and her gaze returned to the bar. Cole was sitting alone, staring into his beer. The brunette must have given up.

As if he felt her gaze, he looked over, straight into her eyes. A thrum ran through her, and he hadn't even touched her.

It was really getting annoying. And it was time to do something about it.

"I'm a little tired," she said to her friends around the table. No lie there. "I think I'll be going now."

Nathan said, "Could I give you a ride home?"

Nathan Hampton wasn't at all hard on the eyes. And he was earnest and friendly and interested. He was good with children, and who loved animals more than a veterinarian? He was easy to talk to and seemed to be an all-around good guy. But a few minutes ago his fingers had brushed hers, and it didn't create a single reaction anywhere.

He had a nice smile. He smiled a lot. Unlike someone else she knew, who looked this very minute as if he wanted to chew glass.

"No, thanks," she said to Nathan. "There's something I need to do."

Chelsea, beautiful, sleek and intuitive as always, winked at April. "Go, girl."

April slipped the strap of her purse over her shoulder and strode to the bar full of purposeful intent. Cole saw her coming and didn't take his eyes off her. "I'd like a word with you," she said.

He indicated the empty barstool next to him. But April shook her head. "Someplace more private," she said.

He dropped a twenty-dollar bill on the bar next to his untouched beer. By the time he stood, making certain his feet were firmly under him, she was halfway to the door.

Out in the alley, the door closed behind them, leaving the din of laughter and music inside. It was a beautiful night. Stars were out, as were late dog-walkers and people going from one pub to the next.

"What did you want to talk to me about?" he asked, his voice deep and husky and as seductive and secretive as the night itself.

Shaking herself, she said, "Here's the thing."

Before she could continue, a couple came out the door and three guys went in. She and Cole moved a little farther down the alley. But the movie must have just ended at the theater around the corner. Throngs of people were taking a shortcut through the alley, making it anything but private.

April clamped her mouth shut.

And he said, "Did you drive?"

She shook her head.

"My truck's this way."

He held the door for her. She got in without touching him. When he was behind the wheel, she said, "Do not try to take me home."

Fifteen seconds later—she knew because she literally counted to fifteen—he said, "Where do you want me to take you?"

And out of her mouth came the words, "To your room at the inn."

She held her breath and waited. Whatever he said or did, or didn't say or didn't do, she was ready.

Chapter Eleven

Heat lightning shimmered over the treetops behind the Stone Inn. For a few seconds April could see the structure's multi-gabled roof and turret windows. It was no wonder stories of ghosts had surfaced here, for the inn resembled haunted houses in old Gothic novels.

Relief surged through her over having gotten this far. She hadn't been certain he would agree. In fact, she'd had to ask him if he trusted her, then had to wait interminable seconds for him to nod before she'd explained there was something she needed to say to him and she couldn't say it at home.

Lightning lit up the sky again, and for a moment she glimpsed the chiseled line of his profile. It wasn't the idea of specters that caused her mouth to go dry and her fingers to tremble as she and Cole walked to the inn's large front door. What if she didn't say the right thing? What if she couldn't make Cole see that love was worth fighting for?

He was a soldier at heart. She prayed he would fight for them.

Lights were on in the downstairs rooms, but most of the windows of the second story were dark. Removing a key from his pocket, Cole unlocked the front door. The foyer was empty, as was the large old innkeeper's desk.

Heat emanated from him as they strode up the wide staircase. He carried himself stiffly. She didn't believe it was due to his injury. He'd erected a wall around him, as if he needed it to gird his resolve and strengthen his willpower. What if she couldn't penetrate that wall?

And then they were at his door at the end of the hall. The moment of truth had arrived.

It was her sister who'd suggested April try to talk some sense into Cole but coming here to Cole's room at the inn had been her own idea. So many of her hopes and dreams and memories already filled her house at 404 Baldwin Street. If this didn't go well, she didn't want her memories of it to be there.

"Here we are."

She'd been so lost in her reveries she jumped at Cole's words. She had no idea how long it had been since she'd stepped over the threshold and he'd closed the door behind them.

Glancing around the room, she wished this didn't have to be awkward.

They remained standing, for she was too nervous to sit down.

She took a small breath, wet her lips and faced the

man she'd fallen in love with. "I'm dreaming again," she said.

"Good dreams?" he asked. They stood a pace apart, close enough to reach out and touch if they so chose. But their hands remained at their sides.

She didn't often wear four-inch heels. They made her feel willowy and pretty and tall, but she still had to look up to study his eyes, and what she saw there gave her hope.

She'd thought it had been his first kiss that had brought her senses back to life. Now she realized it was his eyes, deep and brown and filled with knowledge of both the incredible and the harrowing.

"I've been having erotic dreams," she said, answering his question. "You have the starring role. But that isn't what I came here to tell you."

He shifted his weight to his uninjured leg but he didn't back away. A truly courageous man.

"We both stopped dreaming when Jay died. I don't believe it was a coincidence any more than I believe it's a coincidence that we've both started to dream again now." She paused. And because it was important, she added, "Do you?"

He shook his head, although she doubted he wanted to admit it. He was truthful to a fault. They were alike that way.

"The other night you told me you promised Jay you wouldn't try to take his place. I pray you realize Jay would never hold you to that promise. There's room for both of you in my heart."

He opened his mouth, but as she had before, she placed her hand gently on his arm. And standing stock-still, he waited for her to continue.

"Jay would want me to be happy. You make me happy, Cole. He would want you to be happy, too. Do I make you happy, Cole?"

She waited silently for him to reply.

After interminable seconds, he raked his fingers through his hair. Although his hair had grown out a little from his former military cut, he still seemed to be trying to keep everything under strict control. He walked to the desk, to the window and back again. Finally, he returned to April. Heaving a sigh strong enough to break through his own personal lock and key, he began.

"I dreamed of Jay's death a few nights before he died."

She put her hand over her mouth, picturing Jay bleeding.

Taking a shuddering breath, she touched her fingertip to the line that had formed between Cole's eyes. "That must have been horrible for you."

"For me?" He started pacing again. "We had our orders. He was supposed to stay back, dammit. Then I would have—"

He let his statement go unfinished, but she didn't. "Then you would have been the one to die?"

He clamped his mouth shut, his jaw set.

"Are you sorry you're alive?" she asked.

"Of course not. I'm sorry he isn't!"

"I'm sure you were an outstanding soldier, Cole."

He folded his arms, as if he knew he wasn't going to like what she had to say next.

"I think you feel guilty because Jay died instead of you."

"So?" he said. "He had a helluva lot more to lose than I did."

"Do you know what else I think?" she asked, completely ignoring his outburst. "I think you've mourned Jay even more than I have." She heard him draw a deep breath, saw his chest expand with it.

"You love him as much as I do. Not all soul mates are lovers, Cole. Some are mothers and daughters, fathers and sons, best friends. Some are brothers in war. I'm the grieving widow, and that has entitled me to mourn openly. You're the brave soldier who has saved countless lives, and had your life saved, too. Don't you see? Your life isn't any less important than Jay's was."

"That isn't the point." His throat convulsed on a swallow.

"I already love you, Cole. Even if the unthinkable happened, and you died one day loving me, and forging a life with me, it would hurt less than if you walk away from everything we could have, all we could be together. Losing someone is horrible, believe me, I know, and so do you, but never loving would be worse."

She was coming to expect the way he spun on his heel and started to pace.

She understood just how deeply he mourned Jay, the pain so real it hurt to breathe, how terrifying losing again was for him. In that moment she experienced a fear of her own. What if Cole's emotional scars ran so deep and strong they kept him from risking that kind of loss again?

She didn't know what she would do if he turned away. "Would you do something for me?" she asked. She placed her hands on either side of his face. "Would you take me to bed?"

He stared into her eyes boldly. "Jay never told me you fight dirty."

"Good. I'd rather you discover my secrets on your own."

He was a soldier at heart, and she could see the battle still raging within him.

He looked haunted. Tormented. He heaved a deep sigh and said, "I do love you, April, but I—"

He stopped himself, as if he was thinking what she was thinking, that there were no disqualifiers when it came to love.

The war within him was almost palpable. When she couldn't stand the suspense a second longer, she said, "And?"

Perhaps he overcame his fear right then. Or maybe he surrendered it. She might never know which it was, for her courageous hero took her hands in his, and placed them on his chest where she could feel his heart beating. And then he brought his mouth to hers. She tipped her head back and accepted his kiss. And the man could kiss. Each kiss was a work of art, probably because the emotions behind his kisses came from a place deep inside him where no other woman had ever been allowed entry.

The touch of his mouth on hers extinguished her fears and started a fire inside her. She kissed him in return, drawing his love from him and giving hers back again.

Her emotions made her bold, his touch made her eager. But this was not a man to be rushed. He brought her left hand to his lips, and kissed the indentation where Jay's ring had been. "I noticed you took it off. You don't have to for me."

A tear trailed down her face.

"I love you, April Avery. I've loved you for a long time. And given the chance I will love you until we're both old and gray. There. Are you happy?"

She smiled through her tears. She was, actually. Very happy.

"I don't know why Jay died and I lived. I don't know why things happen. It's as if I'm here for a reason. When the time is right, and you're ready, will you marry me?"

"I'll marry you, all right," she whispered. "Try to stop me."

And his mouth came down on hers again.

They had a lot to work out. What kind of ring did she want? What kind of wedding? When? What would Gracie and Violet call him? Not Daddy. Jay would forever hold that title. Cole didn't care what they called him, but one day soon they would call him Dad. No one would tell them to. They would decide on their own. And it would make him more proud than any medal of honor he'd ever received.

He led her to his bed, lowered the zipper down the back of that amazing dress.

She stepped out of her dress; he did away with her bra; she unbuttoned his shirt. There was no moonlight tonight; as he kissed her, and touched her, and pleasured her, it seemed fitting that they were making love for the first time beneath a new moon.

She unstrapped her sandals; he made short work of shedding his jeans. When she was wearing only her panties and he was wearing nothing at all, he lowered her to the bed. He saw to protection, for they hadn't discussed whether she wanted more children. He did. He could already see the addition he'd build on the back of the house at 404 Baldwin Street. They would discuss those things and more later, and sometimes they would compromise and other times they would argue. But right now, he kissed her, the love of his life, and silently vowed that he would love her till his dying breath.

She trailed kisses of her own along his jaw, along his chin, down his neck. She moved to his shoulder and continued to press gentle kisses down his chest. She found the wound in his side with her lips, and then she found the scar on his thigh. It was thick and jagged and rigid and deep. She would see it in the light a thousand times, but tonight beneath her ministering in the dark, the ugliness dissolved, the pain diminished, sorrow eased, wounds healed inside and out, his and hers.

He withstood her tenderness as long as he could. And then he rolled her underneath him and brought his mouth to hers.

Somewhere a star exploded in a far-off galaxy. They both felt its vibration in unexplainable ways. They saw its twinkling stardust behind their closed eyelids. And with that explosion, they discovered the simple truth.

There was life. And there was death. And if people were fortunate enough, or brave enough, or determined enough to accept it, through it all, there was love.

Late into the night, Cole and April lay close, her head on his chest. He combed his fingers through her long wavy hair, sometimes he twined his fingers with hers. They talked of their childhoods, laughed about funny memories they shared, made love again, and then again.

A connection had formed the moment they'd met upon Cole's arrival in Orchard Hill. Maybe, deep inside, an unnamed part of him really had fallen in love with her while listening to Jay talk about his life here.

Every day since they'd met in person, their connection had deepened, strengthened, sustaining trust in an unknown future.

She trusted him, and he would honor that trust. She trusted love. And so did he.

Epilogue

It was one of those late summer afternoons that couldn't help but put a smile on April's face. The air in downtown Orchard Hill was balmy, the breeze was gentle, and the freshly mown grass on the town square was fragrant and lush.

She and Cole strolled slowly along the curved walkway by Division Street, Gracie and Violet between them, hand-in-hand-in-hand-in-hand. News had spread of their recent engagement. It seemed everyone they met congratulated them. They kissed April's cheek, patted Gracie's and Violet's pretty heads and practically shook Cole's arm off. Many thanked him for his sacrifice and his service. He accepted their appreciation more readily than he had before, but April suspected he would always be private when it came to his service to his country. He was ever watchful, her soldier, the protector of them all.

She never would have believed she could be so gloriously happy again. She could only imagine what her father would say if he were still here, for planning a wedding to be held in only two weeks' time was something her sister would have done. April didn't want to waste a minute of life waiting when she could be spending it with Cole.

The girls' bedrooms were finished. They'd furnished each room with two twin beds, and the girls always both slept in one room or the other. They didn't like to be apart.

It was a beautiful day. It had rained again, and the flowers growing in the planters beside every doorway had never been more lush and fragrant.

A distant memory flitted through April's mind. It almost felt as if she'd been here before. For some reason she half expected to see her father practicing for his next sermon on the glistening marble steps of the courthouse. He wasn't there, of course, for he'd died ten years ago. Still, she felt his presence with her today.

Feeling as carefree as the cotton candy clouds in the sky, she marveled at the brightly colored benches, the brick-paved sidewalks and the windows that reflected an azure blue sky. Recorded music from a children's choir played over the speakers on every street corner. A small group had gathered around the bronze sculpture of Johnny Appleseed, and two women in silver dresses were rehearsing near the fountain.

Gracie and Violet were happy their mother and Cole were getting married, but all they could talk about was the puppy they'd been promised they could choose after their birthday party tomorrow.

For just a moment, April felt the flutter of trepidation. Unable to pinpoint the source, she met her future husband's gaze over her daughters' chatter. Her heart utterly full, she knew she had nothing to fear.

She could hardly believe she could be this lucky. Cole Cavanaugh turned heads, and yet he had eyes only for her. Some women searched their entire lives to find a good, honest man to love. April had been so incredibly blessed to love two.

Dressed in purple as always, Harriet Ferris came out of a nearby shop. Seeing Cole and April and the girls, she beamed a smile and started toward them, her heels click-clacking on the winding sidewalk.

"Let me see this ring I've heard so much about!" the petite woman of indiscernible age insisted. April raised her hand for a moment in order to show Harriet her new engagement ring.

"Look!" Violet said to her sister.

Without warning, she pulled her hand out of Gracie's, streaked off the sidewalk, past a parked car and into the street where a terrified brown-and-yellow dog was running first one way and then another. April froze as tires screeched and horns honked.

"Violet!" her mother screamed.

Oblivious, Violet followed the dog into oncoming traffic.

More brakes screeched, more horns honked. April screamed again.

Cole was running toward Violet, whose sole attention was on the frightened dog. April grabbed Gracie's hand to keep her from following. He moved like lightning, darting between two parked cars, directly into the path of another that was seconds away from hitting the precious little girl. In that split second before that happened, Cole grabbed her up, dove and rolled out of April's sight. There came the discordant sound of crunching metal, shattering glass and the ominous thud of something hard colliding with flesh and bone.

Gracie was crying and April couldn't let herself faint.

Harriet Ferris's blue eyes were round behind her trifocals. April placed Gracie's hand firmly in the older woman's. "Do not let go of her. Please."

Harriet nodded, and held the child with both hands.

April raced into the street now blocked with cars. The cotton candy clouds darkened, the sun had disappeared, the music had stopped. She had to reach Cole and Violet. *Please, God.*

She sprinted around the first car. Because of its angle, she had to take the long way around the second. Fearing what she would find, she came around the back of a white SUV, and there they were, Cole and Violet and the yellow spotted dog.

Cole was sitting on the pavement, holding Violet tight. Both were scraped up. Both were alive.

Sirens blared. People were there suddenly, and they all seemed to be talking at once. As April's eyes met Cole's, everything, all the discordant sounds and the noxious smell of rubber and exhaust fumes, the disarray, the steaming engine and mangled hood of one car and the dented door of another, all of it disappeared.

A light shone from Cole's eyes to hers. That light transcended space and time and connected them to the very beginning when love was created.

He smiled, her hero who'd saved Violet's life. And Violet said, "Mama, the dog's hurt. We have to help her."

April looked closer at the poor creature that lay prone

and utterly still on the pavement several feet away, its right leg bent at a bad angle, its eyes closed. *Oh, no.*

Violet pushed against Cole's arms. "Let me go. Let me go. She needs me."

Stiffly, Cole found his feet, and with Violet still in his arms he started toward the dog. April went with them, swooping gently to her knees where the dog lay.

"Put me down!" Violet demanded. "I need to pet her."

Cole looked to April for direction. At her nod, he carefully set the little girl on her feet, but didn't release her hand.

Together they bent down. Each of them lay a gentle hand on the still animal's side. She was warm, but April felt no heartbeat.

"Violet, honey," she crooned. "I think she's—"

But Violet remained steadfast. Her little hand stroking the soft fur gently, she said nothing.

Then April saw it: the little brown-and-yellow dog moved her tail. It wasn't strong enough to be considered a wag, but she was alive.

Harriet was there suddenly with Gracie and a policeman, too. "She insisted she had to see Violet and their dog. I couldn't hold her back any longer."

With a nod at Harriet, April took her blond-haired daughter's hand. Gracie bent down on her haunches, too, and touched the dog the same way Violet was touching her. The little dog opened her eyes and looked directly at the girls, the thump of her tail growing stronger. Together the twins smiled.

"Easy," April crooned when the animal struggled to get up, but couldn't.

"Lay still," Violet and Gracie said, mimicking their mother.

Another policeman arrived on the scene. And an ambulance, too.

The paramedics swarmed out, ready to take vitals and names. "Is this your dog?" one of them asked.

"Yes," Violet and Grace said in unison.

April and Cole shared a look. Cole had just saved Violet's life, and tears coursed down April's face.

Actually, this was Nathan Hampton's beloved rescue. He was one of the good guys, guys like Cole and Jay. He loved children and animals. She was certain he loved this dog. Right now, April wanted to make sure the dog was going to live.

Abby Fitzpatrick, one of April's closest friends and a reporter with the local newspaper, was snapping pictures. Everybody who had a phone had taken dozens.

The chief EMT wanted Cole and Violet to get in the ambulance. Cole knew Violet was unharmed, for he'd shielded her with his arms, his body, his heart and his soul.

"We're not hurt," he said. "I would tell you if we were. The car missed us. Other than a few scrapes from rolling across the pavement, my daughter and I are fine."

The tears streaming down April's face continued. Her worst nightmare had nearly come true. This scene was so much like the one she'd dreamed it was unnerving, uncanny, terrifyingly real. She could have lost her daughter today. Or Cole. Or both of them.

But she didn't. All because of Cole, her warrior, her hero. She looked at him and saw him looking back at her. Jay had saved Cole's life that horrible day in the desert. And today Cole had saved Violet's. It was as if Jay had brought Cole to Orchard Hill to do this.

There was a lot of commotion, and later she would try to remember who'd been there and what they'd said. Cole was conferring with the police officer and the EMT in charge.

April didn't know what Cole said, but his request was being granted. He picked up the dog as gently as he could. Ever careful of her front leg, he cradled her in his strong arms and carried her to the waiting ambulance. Holding each of her little girls' hands as if she would never let them go, April, Gracie and Violet climbed in, too.

They made the six o'clock news, where Cole was cited for heroism. Watching it from the waiting room of the animal hospital, April marveled at the miracle she'd been granted.

One of the veterinary assistants attended to Cole's and Violet's scrapes. She applied antiseptic and Band-Aids and deemed them almost as good as new. There were smudges on April's white skirt and a hole in Cole's jeans and dirt on Violet's and Gracie's knees, but none of that mattered. Incredibly, all four of them were unharmed.

Nathan Hampton set Roxie's leg himself. A healer in his own right, he stroked his beloved dog's soft fur, and when she woke up, he gave Violet and Gracie their first birthday gift.

"Roxie's yours," he said solemnly to the two little girls who would turn five tomorrow. "You saved her life. Now she will guard yours."

The pair had accepted the gift and the responsibility

as solemnly as it had been given. "Thank you, but her name isn't Roxie, Dr. Hampton," Violet said.

The kindly veterinarian looked perplexed. And April said, "What is her name, then?"

"It's Spot," Gracie said, matter-of-fact.

April and Cole both shook Nathan's hand, and then Cole carried Spot to his truck. April buckled the girls into their booster seats in the back, and being careful of her cast, Cole settled their new dog between them. "Why did you change her name to Spot?" he asked.

Gracie and Violet exchanged a long look. This time it was Gracie who explained. "Because she looks like a spotted leopard."

From their leather bucket seats, Cole and April looked at one another, in awe because Cole had always perceived Jay as a leopard.

"Are you ever going to tell me what animal I am?" she asked softly.

"You're a great northern loon," he said almost as quietly. "Your song is legendary, calling out across fog-covered lakes before dawn's first light. It was your song that called me home."

Her breath caught, for she'd always loved the mystery and the majesty of the loon. Her heart brimming with thankfulness and love, she lay her hand over his on the shift lever.

Cotton candy clouds dotted the horizon, and even though it was almost September, she felt a breeze that carried the scent of the first dandelion on spring grass and that courageous faint ray of sunshine that melted the last tuft of snow. An instant later it was gone, but Jay's blessing remained with all of them.

Love filled the cab of that pickup truck as Cole very

carefully drove his family home, a man who was a hero, a woman whose love healed, two little girls who'd gotten exactly what they wanted for their birthday and the spotted dog with the cast on her leg and a tail that hadn't stopped wagging since she woke up.

* * * * *

For another heart-touching
look into the lives of the
people in Orchard Hill, read
The Wedding Gift
and don't miss a single story in
the Round-the-Clock Brides series:

A Bride Until Midnight
A Bride Before Dawn
A Bride by Summer

by Sandra Steffen
available from
Harlequin Special Edition.

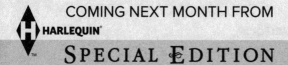

COMING NEXT MONTH FROM

HARLEQUIN®

SPECIAL EDITION

Available October 22, 2019

#2725 MAVERICK HOLIDAY MAGIC
Montana Mavericks: Six Brides for Six Brothers • by Teresa Southwick
Widowed rancher Hunter Crawford will do anything to make his daughter happy—even if it means hiring a live-in nanny he thinks he doesn't need. Merry Matthews quickly fills their house with cookies and Christmas spirit, leaving Hunter to wonder if he might be able to keep this kind of magic forever...

#2726 A WYOMING CHRISTMAS TO REMEMBER
The Wyoming Multiples • by Melissa Senate
Stricken with temporary amnesia, Maddie Wolfe can't remember a single thing about her life...or her husband, Sawyer. But even with electricity crackling between them, it turns out their fairy tale was careening toward disaster. Will a little Christmas spirit help Maddie find her memories—and the Wolfes find the spark again?

#2727 THE SCROOGE OF LOON LAKE
Small-Town Sweethearts • by Carrie Nichols
Former navy lieutenant Desmond "Des" Gallagher has only bad memories of Christmas from his childhood, so he hides away in the workshop of his barn during the holidays. But Natalie Pierce is determined to get his help to save her son's horse therapy program, and Des finds himself drawn to a woman he's not sure he can love the way she needs.

#2728 THEIR UNEXPECTED CHRISTMAS GIFT
The Stone Gap Inn • by Shirley Jump
When a baby shows up in the kitchen of a bed-and-breakfast, chef Nick Jackson helps the baby's aunt, Vivian Winthrop, create a makeshift family to give little Ellie a perfect Christmas. But playing family together might get more serious than either of them thought it could...

#2729 A DOWN-HOME SAVANNAH CHRISTMAS
The Savannah Sisters • by Nancy Robards Thompson
The odds of Ellie Clark falling for Daniel Quindlin are slim to none. First, she isn't home to stay. And second, Daniel caused Ellie's fiancé to leave her at the altar. Even if he had her best interests at heart, falling for her archnemesis just isn't natural. Well, neither is a white Christmas in Savannah...

#2730 HOLIDAY BY CANDLELIGHT
Sutter Creek, Montana • by Laurel Greer
Avalanche survivor Dr. Caleb Matsuda is intent on living a risk-free life. But planning a holiday party with free-spirited mountain rescuer Garnet James tempts the handsome doctor to take a chance on love.

HSECNM1019

Stricken with temporary amnesia, Maddie Wolfe can't remember a single thing about her life...or her husband, Sawyer. But even with electricity crackling between them, it turns out their fairy tale was careening toward disaster. Will a little Christmas spirit help Maddie find her memories—and the Wolfes find the spark again?

Read on for a sneak preview of
A Wyoming Christmas to Remember
by Melissa Senate,
the next book in the Wyoming Multiples miniseries.

"Three weeks?" she repeated. "I might not remember anything about myself for three weeks?"

Dr. Addison gave her a reassuring smile. "Could be sooner. But we'll run some tests, and based on how well you're doing now, I don't see any reason why you can't be discharged later today."

Discharged where? Where did she live?

With your husband, she reminded herself.

She bolted upright again, her gaze moving to Sawyer, who pocketed his phone and came back over, sitting down and taking her hand in both of his. "Do I—do we—have children?" she asked him. She couldn't forget her own children. She couldn't.

"No," he said, glancing away for a moment. "Your parents and Jenna will be here in fifteen minutes," he said. "They're ecstatic you're awake. I let them know you might not remember them straightaway."

"Jenna?" she asked.

"Your twin sister. You're very close. To your parents, too. Your family is incredible—very warm and loving."

That was good.

She took a deep breath and looked at her hand in his. Her left hand. She wasn't wearing a wedding ring. He wore one, though—a gold band. So where was hers?

"Why aren't I wearing a wedding ring?" she asked.

His expression changed on a dime. He looked at her, then down at his feet. Dark brown cowboy boots.

Uh-oh, she thought. *He doesn't want to tell me. What is that about?*

Two orderlies came in just then, and Dr. Addison let Maddie know it was time for her CT scan, and that by the time she was done, her family would probably be here.

"I'll be waiting right here," Sawyer said, gently cupping his hand to her cheek.

As the orderlies wheeled her toward the door, she realized she missed Sawyer—looking at him, talking to him, her hand in his, his hand on her face. That had to be a good sign, right?

Even if she wasn't wearing her ring.

Don't miss
A Wyoming Christmas to Remember
by Melissa Senate,
available November 2019 wherever
Harlequin® Special Edition books and ebooks are sold.

www.Harlequin.com

Get 4 FREE REWARDS!

We'll send you 2 FREE Books plus 2 FREE Mystery Gifts.

Harlequin® Special Edition books feature heroines finding the balance between their work life and personal life on the way to finding true love.

FREE
Value Over
$20

YES! Please send me 2 FREE Harlequin® Special Edition novels and my 2 FREE gifts (gifts are worth about $10 retail). After receiving them, if I don't wish to receive any more books, I can return the shipping statement marked "cancel." If I don't cancel, I will receive 6 brand-new novels every month and be billed just $4.99 per book in the U.S. or $5.74 per book in Canada. That's a savings of at least 12% off the cover price! It's quite a bargain! Shipping and handling is just 50¢ per book in the U.S. and $1.25 per book in Canada.* I understand that accepting the 2 free books and gifts places me under no obligation to buy anything. I can always return a shipment and cancel at any time. The free books and gifts are mine to keep no matter what I decide.

235/335 HDN GNMP

Name (please print)

Address   Apt. #

City   State/Province   Zip/Postal Code

Mail to the **Reader Service:**
IN U.S.A.: P.O. Box 1341, Buffalo, NY 14240-8531
IN CANADA: P.O. Box 603, Fort Erie, Ontario L2A 5X3

Want to try 2 free books from another series? Call 1-800-873-8635 or visit www.ReaderService.com.

HSE20

SPECIAL EXCERPT FROM

Seven years ago, Elizabeth Hamilton ran away from her family. Now she's back to end things permanently, only to discover how very much she wants to stay. Can the hurt of the past seven years be healed over the course of one Christmas season and bring the Hamiltons the gift of a new beginning?

Turn the page for a sneak peek at
New York Times *bestselling author RaeAnne Thayne's heartwarming Haven Point story*
Coming Home for Christmas, *available now!*

This was it.

Luke Hamilton waited outside the big rambling Victorian house in a little coastal town in Oregon, hands shoved into the pockets of his coat against the wet slap of air and the nerves churning through him.

Elizabeth was here. After all the years when he had been certain she was dead—that she had wandered into the mountains somewhere that cold day seven years earlier or she had somehow walked into the deep, unforgiving waters of Lake Haven—he was going to see her again.

Though he had been given months to wrap his head around the idea that his wife wasn't dead, that she was indeed living under another name in this town by the sea, it still didn't seem real.

How was he supposed to feel in this moment? He had no idea. He only knew he was filled with a crazy mix of anticipation, fear and the low fury that had been simmering inside him for months, since the moment FBI agent Elliot Bailey had produced a piece of paper with a name and an address.

Luke still couldn't quite believe she was in there—the wife he had not seen in seven years. The wife who had disappeared off the face of the earth, leaving plenty of people to speculate that he had somehow hurt her, even killed her.

For all those days and months and years, he had lived with the ghost of Elizabeth Sinclair and the love they had once shared.

He was never nervous, damn it. So why did his skin itch and his stomach seethe and his hands grip the cold metal of the porch railing as if his suddenly weak knees would give way and make him topple over if he let go?

A moment later, he sensed movement inside the foyer of the house. The woman he had spoken with when he had first pulled up to this address, the woman who had been hanging Christmas lights around the big charming home and who had looked at him with such suspicion and had not invited him to wait inside, opened the door. One hand was thrust into her coat pocket around a questionable-looking bulge.

She was either concealing a handgun or a Taser or pepper spray. Since he was not familiar with the woman, Luke couldn't begin to guess which. Her features had lost none of that alert wariness that told him she would do whatever necessary to protect Elizabeth.

He wanted to tell her he would never hurt his wife, but it was a refrain he had grown tired of repeating. Over the years, he had become inured to people's opinions on the matter. Let them think what the hell they wanted. He knew the truth.

"Where is she?" he demanded.

There was a long pause, like that tension-filled moment just before the gunfight in Old West movies. He wouldn't have been surprised if tumbleweeds suddenly blew down the street.

Then, from behind the first woman, another figure stepped out onto the porch, slim and blonde and…shockingly familiar.

He stared, stunned to his bones. It was her. Not Elizabeth. *Her*. He had seen this woman around his small Idaho town of Haven Point several times over the last few years, fleeting glimpses only out of the corner of his gaze at a baseball game or a school program.

The mystery woman.

Don't miss
Coming Home for Christmas *by RaeAnne Thayne,*
available wherever
HQN books and ebooks are sold!